R.E. Bowden is a Senior Lecturer in Visual Communications at Wolverhampton University, now retired. Robert taught students on a BA (Honours) course in Graphic Design.

Outside of his career, he is a keen boater and musician, acting as Musical Director for some ten shows and a member of a band. He has written several folk songs about narrow boating on canals and rivers. He is also a keen modeller and enthusiast for the hobby of model railways.

He has now written five novels, including a science fiction comedy and a children's adventure set in Animal World.

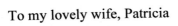
To my lovely wife, Patricia

R.E. Bowden

THE GIRL ON A BIKE

AUSTIN MACAULEY PUBLISHERS™

LONDON · CAMBRIDGE · NEW YORK · SHARJAH

A CIP catalogue record for this title is available from the British Library.

ISBN 9781398497290 (Paperback)
ISBN 9781398497306 (ePub e-book)

www.austinmacauley.com

First Published 2023
Austin Macauley Publishers Ltd®
1 Canada Square
Canary Wharf
London
E14 5AA

Thanks to the editorial staff for knocking my poor story into something worth publishing!

Part One
Kylie

Chapter One

Kylie, a pretty 12-year-old girl, her long blonde hair tied in a ponytail, was delivering newspapers on her bike. It was 07:21 on a pleasant early spring Monday morning. The newspaper round Kylie had was mainly focused on housing estates in the immediate area, but there was a small section of fairly-isolated country lanes, where the houses were large, scattered on the edge of the town.

Kylie, labouring uphill, noticed a small white van, with a sign on the rear doors stating **AB Landscape Gardeners** parked at the side of one of such narrow lanes, half onto a grass verge. As she pulled over to overtake, the driver's door swung open and a man in a white coat lunged out of the van, forcing Kylie to swerve and fall onto the opposite verge, which was covered with thick weeds and long grass, cushioning her fall.

She started to scream but he quickly bent over her and applied a pad soaked in ether over her mouth and nose. Kylie almost immediately slumped and went limp. The man, who was young and athletic, easily picked her up and placed her gently on bedding in the back of his van. He took her phone, switched it off and placed it in a metal box. He then went and picked up her pink bicycle and put that in his van also, on a plastic sheet.

He looked about and noted with satisfaction that there were no onlookers around. He carefully examined the verge where the girl had fallen and made sure there were no tell-tale marks. He took a rake out of the van and made extra sure. He then, without haste, got in his van and drove carefully off. The whole thing had taken no more than five minutes. The man was smiling in anticipation of what lay ahead for him.

At 10:30 am the same morning, Kylie's class teacher, while on her tea break, rang Kylie's mum Carol, because Kylie was never late and never ill, so she was concerned about her. She knew Carol quite well as they were both in a gym class, doing Tai Chi twice a week. Carol panicked immediately. She knew Kylie had gone on her newspaper round and that she always went to school straight after delivering her papers and did not return home until the afternoon when school ended for the day.

Carol phoned around the newsagent, her mother, her friends, without result. The newsagent told her that he had got some angry customers who had not got their morning papers, from Kylie's round. At 11:15 she rang the school again to see if her daughter had arrived. She hadn't and the headteacher advised Carol to ring the police. Trembling with anguish, she did. The police receptionist asked for some details and then told Carol to stay in her home and that someone would call around shortly to take a statement.

Half an hour later, a smart young lady detective called, dressed in a black skirt and a white jumper. Her name was Detective Constable Penny Summers, who introduced herself, showed her ID and said she had come about the missing girl.

Carol showed Penny into her front room and asked her to sit down, indicating a massive comfy-looking armchair, where her husband usually sat. Penny perched herself as best she could, as a five-foot small, solidly-built woman could manage.

"So, your daughter's name is Kylie Patricia and she is twelve years old. Is that right, Mrs Thomas?" asked DC Penny, taking out her notebook from her briefcase.

Carol nodded her head. She sat twisting her hands in her lap. She had obviously been crying.

She said, croakily, "She's nearly thirteen and she's well developed for her age if you know what I mean. It's her birthday next month, the 10th. Christ!" Her eyes opened very wide, as she had an awful thought, *Would she be alive to enjoy her first year as a teenager?*

"I know this is horrible for you, Mrs Thomas, but *do* try to stay calm. I'm sure your daughter will turn up unharmed. In ninety-nine cases out of a hundred, kids always turn up eventually and have just wandered off somewhere, distracted by something that has taken their fancy or whatever. Don't you worry, there's really no need at this stage, honestly. Now then, what time was it the last time you saw her?"

"It was 7 o'clock this morning when she went off on her bike to deliver her paper round. The newsagent, Mr Khan, told me that some of the houses on her round had not received their morning papers, so she didn't finish her round." Carol's voice was struggling and weak with emotion. Penny could only just hear her.

"Mm, so it appears she went somewhere else, rather than finishing her round and then, maybe, she has been delayed by something happening to cause her to stop delivering papers. It seems very odd, I must say."

Penny, writing in her notebook, looked concerned. She was wearing rather a short skirt and black tights and had short and rather plump legs. She pulled her skirt down as far as it would go, in an unconscious gesture. The chair was much too large for her and her feet did not touch the carpeted floor so she wished she could kick off her sensible shoes and tuck her legs under her—but knew it would be unprofessional. This did not usually deter her much.

Carol said, urgently, leaning forwards, "She really isn't the type of girl to just go off on a whim. She knows all about the dangers of talking to strangers. I've drilled that into her time and time again." Her voice rose, "There's no way she's just gone off somewhere unless something really horrible has happened. I can't imagine what it could be."

I think my Kylie has been abducted, I really do! Christ! Carol's face was deep red and she was shouting hysterically, she had risen from her chair and was standing right in front of the young constable in an aggressive posture, arms akimbo. A chiming clock rang out on the fireplace surround, adding an incongruous note, like the end of a round of boxing.

Penny held up her hands, "Alright, calm down, this won't help!"

"Calm down! Are you serious? Some bastard has abducted my bleeding daughter and you tell me to calm down! Why aren't you out there searching for her? I'm not sitting here any longer constable, I'm going out to look for her and that's what you should be doing, damn you!" Carol started for the door, bursting into tears. Penny managed to squirm herself out of the massive chair and stood up.

14

"OK. OK. Look, I'm sorry. Of course, you're really, really upset. Of course, you are, but if we are to help you, we need more information. Have you searched this house? Sometimes kids just hide away, you know, it's quite common if they are upset. Have you been having trouble with Kylie? It's a difficult age."

Carol was blazing. She shouted, "No! I haven't searched the bleedin' house!"

Penny grabbed the shaking woman by the shoulders, held her in a strong grip and said, firmly, "We must follow procedures, we will need to search your house and the garage and the garden and the loft, everywhere, before we widen the search. Then we will search the school premises because that's another place where kids often hide themselves if they are troubled in some way. After that, we will put together a full search team to scour the immediate area. It is all standard procedure and it works well time after time, Mrs Thomas. Look, it won't help your daughter flying off the handle, you will really have to stay in your house in case Kylie returns here in the next few hours. She has only been missing a few hours, love, but she is a young child and we must act quickly and do the best we can to find her and bring her back to you safe and sound."

"Now, to work. Have you got a recent picture of Kylie we can have? Can you describe exactly what she was wearing when she left this morning? Who is her best friend? Has she got a boyfriend—it's not unknown at her age, you know—all these things are vitally important, Mrs Thomas. *Vitally important*."

"I have to write a report for the Inspector. I need her phone number and the make and type of her mobile. If her phone is switched on we can locate it, you know? I suppose, of course, you have tried ringing her many times?"

Carol was slumped in Penny's arms. She nodded her head, unable to reply. She sat down again for a minute, trying to compose herself, then went out and returned with a school photo of her daughter in her school uniform, looking absolutely gorgeous and smart. She handed it over to the young detective and apologised for 'losing her rag' as she put it. She had brought with her a small glass of brandy, which she sipped from, saying, "I need this."

After a few seconds, Carol started to speak again, quickly, almost gabbling, "She hasn't got a boyfriend, as far as I know, Constable. She goes around with a group of school friends, girls and boys, she hasn't got a special friend, I don't think. I don't know who they are really. She's very bossy, you know. Her phone is the latest iPhone and in a pink case. Look, this is her number in my address book."

"You must look for her bicycle. It's pink and nearly new, it must be lying somewhere on her newspaper round route, but I'm not sure what that is, that's unless the swine who took her took her bike as well. She was wearing her school uniform, under a pink coat, a shiny pink weatherproof one with a hood, from Next? She wears a strip of reflective tape on her back, like, so she is easy to see on the road from behind."

"She's never had an accident, she rides very carefully, you know. She's such a good girl, no trouble, very bright, good at all her subjects at school, which she loves. She plays football with the lad's team, a real tomboy that one! Noisy too. *Loud*. Always laughing and joking and bounding about. The house will be so quiet without her—" Carol's voice had tailed off and she could not go on. She just sat and sobbed her heart out, wailing and shivering uncontrollably.

"Do you have someone who will come and stay with you, Mrs Thomas?" asked Penny quietly, holding the shaking woman closely. Someone was banging furiously on the front door.

"Yes," gasped Carol, "My mum is on the way over—in fact, I think that's her now." She ran to open the door. She and her mum hugged each other, both clearly very upset. Penny took the opportunity to do a quick, but thorough, search of the house. She pulled down the built-in ladder in the loft as well and peered in. No sign. She raced around and looked through the garage window; empty. She knew it was all a waste of time, but, it had to be done. Procedures.

It then took the young detective another half an hour to get Mrs Thomas to answer all her questions to her satisfaction. At last, she stood up.

She said, "Thank you, Mrs Thomas. I have all I need for now. I will go back to the station and get things moving. I'm sure your daughter will turn up soon and if she does, don't forget to give me a ring. Here's my card. You can ring me any time you like. Now, you try to relax, you must look after yourself you know, if only for Kylie's sake. I'll be in touch later today. Oh, can I have a quick look around the garden and the garage?"

Carol nodded, quieter now she had her mum's support. They both stood up and watched as Penny left the room. They looked shattered, as well they might.

Chapter Two

Detective Constable Penny Summers returned to the station and after having a session with her sergeant, Albert Phipps, (known as 'Phippy'), went to see her boss, Detective Inspector Michael Carter, who was in his office struggling with a mountain of paperwork, as usual. He looked up as she entered and smiled. He liked and respected the young woman, who was a real asset to the force.

He said, "Hiya, Pen. Gee babe! You look durn prettier every time I see ya!" in an awful parody of an American accent, taken from his addiction to the most lurid American detective thrillers on the cinema and TV. Nothing annoyed Penny more, but he was totally unaware of it. She, however, fancied him like mad. That, he *was* aware of and he basked in it! They often worked closely together, because they both liked it that way and they sparked off each other to good effect.

"What can I *do you for*, kid?" he jokingly asked.

She ignored this nonsense as best as she could. "Sir," she said, "We have a problem. A child, a 12-year-old, named Kylie Thomas, described by her mum as being well-developed—and actually she is nearly thirteen—anyway, she has gone missing, under very suspicious circumstances and I am worried about her safety. It is very probable that she has been abducted."

Mike immediately changed his attitude. His boyishly handsome face became very serious. He listened intently while Penny told him about her visit to Kylie's home in a short, but accurate report.

"Crikey Moses, Pen, this is not good news. You had better get a team together right away and do all the necessary. You know the drill, constable."

"Yes, sir. I've already made a start. Phippy has taken three uniforms to the school to do a search of the place and the grounds. I have done a quick search of the missing girl's home and garden, etc. As far as I can tell, she is not hiding away."

Mike said, "Right, good work. Yes, the fact that she did not finish her paper round is really worrying me. I mean, where are the missing papers? Where is her bike? It does not look good, as you rightly say, Pen. I have a nasty gut feeling about this. I really do. Can the forensic guys get a fix on her phone, I wonder?" He added, grimly, "Shit!"

He picked up the next document from the pile in front of him and banged it on his desk. "It's the last thing we damn well want!"

Penny said nothing. She turned on her heel and headed for the door.

Mike looked up. "Keep me informed, Pen," he said.

As soon as she had left, he picked up his phone to book an appointment with his immediate boss, Detective Chief Superintendent Len Rowles, a huge man with a permanently red, misshapen large nose, leading to his nickname 'Rudolph'. He was respected, liked, but feared in equal measures by his staff. They knew that when the Super was angry, they better look out! He and DI Mike Carter, however, got on well with each other through mutual respect and friendship.

The team had had many other instances, of course, of children going missing. It was a regular occurrence. There were well-established and practised procedures in place that were always strictly followed. Reports had to be written. Relevant bodies had to be consulted and informed. It was routine. Just another day in Wolverhampton's old city, founded by the Abbess, Lady Wulfruna in the tenth-century and now a large multi-cultural hub where over a hundred different languages were spoken in the streets and estates.

Petty crime was common and success in solving them rates were low, less than ten per cent. This was more or less the average overall the country. In the city, serious crime was fairly rare, however and this had a much better resolution rate. There were five murders ongoing at the time and the team confidently expected to clear these up eventually, with suspects in custody for three of them, all partners of the ones' murdered, as is common.

Chapter Three

One Year Previously

The Annual Masonic Ladies' Dinner and Dance were in full swing at the top hotel in the city. One corner of the banqueting room was particularly lively. The couple who were the centre of attraction, as usual, were holding forth with their witty repartee, surrounded by a posse of ardent admirers. Maggie Shaw was the star of the show, again as usual. A magnetic woman, glamorous and beautiful in a shimmering gold dress showing off her ample charms.

Her escort, the young, floppy-haired and remarkably-handsome consultant surgeon and professor of medicine, Dr Prof. Simon Shaw. What most people in the room did not know was that Simon was actually Maggie's son, not her husband, which people naturally assumed, as the lady looked so vital and young, belying her mid-forties age group. She had given birth to Simon when she was only fourteen years of age, the victim of a fat, lecherous politician.

The whole incident had been hushed up and Maggie had been whisked off to a very exclusive Swiss clinic for the birth to avoid a scandal for her very upper-class super-rich family.

Simon adored his mother and the feeling was mutual. Neither wanted anyone else. Maggie, resulting from her dreadful experience as a teenager, held men in general in contempt, though fortunately, she was able to mask this in the company. Simon brought up without a father figure and aware of his mother's feelings, had no desire for a female company other than his doting mother.

Many young ladies had set their hearts on catching him as a husband, but they had no chance at all. He just ignored all advances, with a shy smile that sent such ladies into frustrated raptures!

For Simon and his mother, everything was perfect. Paradise on earth for over thirty years—

Present Day

Dr Prof. Simon Shaw had just returned home, after driving just over two miles into the edge of the Shropshire countryside. He lived in a Victorian red-brick mansion, built for a very rich merchant in the wool trade. It had ten bedrooms, all *en-suite* and four large reception rooms, a fabulous mirrored ballroom, complete with chandeliers, copied from Versailles, a dining room, a billiards room, a vast kitchen, extensive wine cellar below ground and a massively-beautiful conservatory/orangery, looking out onto a nine-acre garden.

At the far end of the garden, hidden from the mansion by trees, was a futuristic-looking single-story rambling house where Maggie Shaw had lived, before her tragic demise. She had designed the house herself and it had won several awards. The views of the Shropshire Hills in the distance were stunning—*those blue-remembered hills*—as beautifully described in A. E. Housman's collection of poems: *A Shropshire Lad.*

Maggie's home was the ultimate in smart technology and utter luxury. It also reflected her passion for music. An accomplished pianist herself, she had included in her home a good-sized concert hall, where she invited the local 'great and good' to come and listen to some of the well-known artists of the classical world in an atmosphere of champagne and gourmet picnics, a much-cherished part of the local high society genre.

Simon attended all the concerts. He was also a fine musician and a conductor. They often played duets on two pianos, of music arranged by themselves. They also danced, as both were madly passionate about Ballet. They had both been privately trained as ballet dancers all their lives and had reached a professional standard and both served as Artistic Directors of a local ballet company. They were praised for their beautiful *pas-de-deux.*

After a performance, he usually slept in his mother's home. Rumour had it that it was in the same bed—untrue.

Those wonderful events were all, sadly, now no more. The building was empty and forlorn, its' windows boarded up, its' doors permanently closed. When Maggie died a light had gone out in the area that would never be lit again.

Maggie had died as a result of a traffic accident, some months ago. She had been riding her powerful Honda motorbike at night on the M6 motorway. The police estimated she was doing well over 100 miles an hour when her front tyre had burst, launching her off an elevated stretch of the road and into a derelict stone farm building which had stood there for hundreds of years.

When Simon was told of the death of his mother, his reaction had been just to remain silent, wooden-faced. There was no show of grief He simply walked out of the room. But Simon, at that hour, died inside. He was totally bereft and inconsolable, his whole personality changed and a monster was set free.

It was Simon who brought Kylie home that day in the small, white van he had bought for the purpose. He had installed a sensor in the cab which opened automatically the gates of his estate. However, he drove past the house where he lived and further on in the estate, towards another building, again a futuristic design, which was designed as a private leisure centre, based on a modern interpretation of an ancient Roman Baths, containing a large heated pool, hot rooms, cold rooms, a gymnasium and several exotic pleasure rooms, as his mother called them.

Modern showers and toilets replaced the lavatoria of old, thankfully. Fancy dress parties were held here, often with an Ancient Roman theme. Actors were hired to play slaves, bacchanalian feasting followed. Wine and grapes flowed continually. Nudity was insisted upon, as per ancient roman practice. No sex was allowed—and, oddly, no one ever complained. Their parties took place on Sunday afternoons and continued all night.

The main problem for guests was that Maggie and her son were both strict Vegans, Naturists and Health and Fitness devotees. Their parties excluded any meat or smoking as well as sex! Nudity was essential. Welcome were children and dogs, but not cats. Maggie could not stand tomcats. They still had lots of similar-minded friends or weirdos, as some of the uninvited called them!

Invitations were highly sought after among the upper-class locals. Most of their friends were, despite this, doctors, musicians, actors, ballet dancers, poets, writers and the like. They liked to think they were the Intelligencia—and perhaps they were.

Music to suit all moods was available for each room in a vast choice. It had sleeping accommodation and was fitted with many electronic devices, including giant wall screens which could be programmed to simulate mountain views, forest views, beach views, etc. The air conditioning could simulate sea breezes or mountain freshness, all with accompanying aromas, of pine, ozone, etc.

The whole building was designed for hedonistic pleasure and had been well-used by Maggie and her upper-class friends until her untimely death. Now only Kylie would be there. It was all part of Simon's grand plan.

He carried the young girl, still unconscious, into one of the so-called pleasure rooms, fitted with soft silk leisure loungers and every known means of electronic entertainment on tap. The walls were covered in silk drapes and a vast triple-glazed window looked out over the distant Shropshire hills. It had been his mother's favourite room. He laid Kylie down on a white silk-covered leather lounger, where Maggie had often relaxed. He gave her a cursory medical examination, followed by an injection of Rohypnol. He estimated she would sleep for at least another twelve hours before waking up.

Satisfied, he removed her coat and her school uniform and dressed her in a white silk onesie, bought, with lots of other clothes, on the net for the girl, estimating her size correctly. He took no notice of her body, apart from approving her obvious physical fitness. Sex did not enter his mind at all. She was, after all, a child and he a doctor, well-used to nude bodies of all shapes, ages and sizes. And he was a naturist, as noted.

Simon, well satisfied with his work, left the room to the strains of Saint-Saen's *Claire du Lune*, recorded and played by his mother on the piano, one of her favourite studies. He returned to his house, where he sat in his favourite chair, a soft full-lipped smile on his round, boyish face, his mass of dark brown curly hair tousled around his beautiful head. He was at peace. At last.

A large screen on the wall showed a live picture of Kylie, lying where his mother had so often lain. The picture kept changing angles and included a close-up of her sleeping face. Simon just gazed and gazed. He was in a personal Heaven. He had so many plans. So many dreams. And they were all coming true.

Chapter Four

At the station, the team were assembled for their 10 am briefing. Around the room were display boards with each board showing photographs, documents, notes, diagrams, maps, etc, etc. Each board represented a current investigation of the more serious crimes. Mike and Phippy went from board to board, detailing the current status and progress and allocating staff to various tasks that needed attention.

A new board had been started, labelled **Missing Child— Kylie Thomas**. So far, the only picture was a copy of the school portrait given to Penny by Mrs Carol Thomas, the victim's mother. Penny's report was also pinned up alongside, together with a section of a large-scale OS map.

DS Phipps addressed the team. A large section of a local OS map was also on show, with a red line displaying Kylie's newspaper round route. A large star indicated one road in particular.

"Royt! A new case here and royt bastard of a case guys." Detective Sergeant Albert Phipps, known to everyone as 'Phippy' was a black country man through and through, born in Cradley Heath, once the site of a huge steelworks, now well gone, like the vast majority of the heavy engineering works that once employed thousands and made this area the workshop of the world. Phippy spoke with a pronounced black country accent—

"So wharrav we'm got? A missing choyld. Twelve years of age, described as being well-developed for her age and yow all know what that means. All royt, all royt!" He glared as some sniggers were heard from the males, "Grow up yow wankers! This'm a choyld! Alright, she'm nearly thirteen and a looker and this is really bloody worrying.

There's plenty of paedos round 'ere as yow all know, who'd give them royt arms to have this lass to play with. It looks loike er's been abducted. She went missing some way short of the end of 'er paper round. Now—we sorta know where she went missing and when. She did not deliver her papers after leaving the estate here on this map."

Phippy pointed and waited for the team's heads to nod, then he continued, "this lane 'ere, Bluebell Lane, is where she must 'ave been taken, loike. It's hilly, narra and twisty, as yow can see. The perpetrator must have somehow got the young lass to goo with 'im, presumably in 'is vehicle and as he must have taken 'er bike as well and the rest of the papers. He may well have assaulted the girl and knocked 'er out, we don't know.

The 'ouses on Bluebell Lane are few and far between, mostly farm 'ouses or ex-farm 'ouses or just grite big 'ouses with lots a land rund 'em. Only ten of 'em in all and not one of 'em got they'm papers. Some of yow will know we have searched Bluebell Lane from one end to the other, by finger-tip searching, but could we find anything? Sweet FA! Absolutely nowt. We'll do another search and another search, we will keep troying but don't 'old yer breath.

Of course, we don't rayly know if she were abducted at all—it's all in Penny's griyt report pinned up 'ere. We've searched 'er 'ouse and the school, all the usual stuff. Now we'm gooin' ta 'ave to widen it to the local area and call in volunteer 'elp. Royt? That's it! Over to yow. Questions—and I want plenty!"

Taffy, one of the brightest young detectives on the team, put up his hand. He was not popular, having been put on a fast-track career, heading for the top, with a first-class honours degree in Law under his belt. His full name was DC Ivor Parry, LLB. He was hard-working, aggressive and lacked a sense of humour.

Phippy asked, sarcastically, "Ar, yer 'onour?" which got a laugh.

Taffy knew to ignore such remarks. He said, in his lilting Welsh voice, "See you, Sarge, it looks like you've made a great start. I just wondered, see, if we should get a load of photos of young Kylie to put around the route she took that morning. You know, sarge, attached to lamp-posts, gates, windows, sort of thing, asking for information and such."

Taffy was from Ruthin, in North Wales and Welsh was his first language growing up, but he had married a local Wolverhampton girl and they were now engaged in house hunting in the area. A baby was on its' way. He was quite small, 5'6" and stocky, with a fierce-looking jutting black beard. Like lots of small men, he was insanely ambitious.

Phippy said, "Ar, royt, but we'm already got that sorted, Taff, still, bostin' work, lad!" he beamed benevolently. He thought the young Welshman was an arrogant young puppy, too big for his boots, but he would give praise where it was due and he knew the kid was really bright and potentially a really first-class detective when he had matured a bit and got the rough edges knocked off. No real malice in Phippy's body.

Everybody, including Taffy himself, liked Phippy. He was an institution. Very tall, very thin and bony with a long face that looked permanently glum. However, his true nature was kindly and helpful—he was recognised as a great copper of the old school. His knowledge of police procedures was legendary. If there was a problem—ask Phippy!

Another member of the team, a newcomer, put his hand up. Phippy smiled benignly at him. "Orlroyt, kidder, what y'om tinkin? Spake up!"

"Has she been kidnapped, sarge? Or abducted, trafficked or what?"

DCI Mike, butted in, "I'll answer this one, Phippy, thanks for the question, Robbie, it needed asking, Son. I doubt very much whether it's a kidnapping because the family is not rich by any means, just an ordinary family of hardworking folk, trying to make ends meet, pay the rent or the mortgage and living on or near the edge, like most of us, especially now we have got this damn pandemic to cope with.

No, Son, it must be either an abduction or she has just gone off on her bike somewhere, maybe just done a runner. I'm hoping that is the case, although there is no evidence to suggest she would do such a thing. Of course, she could be dead, her body hidden away somewhere. God only knows. We may never know the truth, sadly."

Constable Robbie Forsyth looked pleased with himself. He was a huge young man with ginger hair, a cheeky face and a bad case of acne. All his spare time he was in the gym, practising weight-lifting and body building. He was an awesome sight oiled up and in his faux leopard skin posing pouch! 6'7" and 18 stone of toned muscle. Known among his friends as a 'gentle giant'.

DC Summers also raised her small, well-shaped hand.

"Ar?" asked the sergeant.

"I don't think there is any possibility of Kylie just going off on her bicycle. I have talked to her mum and her nan and to her class teacher and some of her many friends and they all say she no way would have left home. She is a popular and well-liked girl, who 'would do anything for anyone' as they say. She is well-settled at school and never in any trouble.

She does not have a boyfriend and in fact, she does not seem to want to bother with boys at all, except to play football with—or many other sports—a real athlete, good at everything apparently. It might be significant but she does suffer from asthma occasionally and needs an inhaler to control any of the rare attacks and her mum says she forgot to take it with her.

A lovely young girl, Kylie, full of fun, kind-hearted and generous—a really nice kid by all accounts. I'm sorry to say it really looks like what her mum suspects is the truth—some bastard has carried her off, bike, papers and all. That's all I want to say, sir."

"Ar, yo'm royt theer, ar kid," said Phippy, slowly and dolefully.

Then, "Thank you, Penny," said both the inspector and the sergeant together. Penny looked close to tears and had gone red with emotion.

Robbie, who had a soft spot for Penny, put up an enormous hand, like a shovel; he didn't wait, he just shouted out, "The bugger must have had a van or a big estate car, sir,

I wish I could have five minutes alone with the swine." (Not so gentle after all, then). There were murmurs of agreement.

Phippy just nodded his long head and looked even more gloomy than ever. He cautioned, "Let's kayp this on a professional level, kidder." But it was obvious he really totally agreed with Robbie's sentiment—He added, "Ar. Yo'm royt, lad, he must 'ave 'ad a van or somat. Well done. Any more questions?"

"Send for Rudi!" someone shouted, to general laughter. Rudi or Dr Rudolph Valentine, to give him his proper name, was the FBI Profiler who had helped the team solve the "Angel of Death" case a year or so earlier.

Mike did not join in the laughter, he looked thoughtful. Then he said, "As far as looking for the vehicle is concerned, there are no cameras anywhere on Kylie's newspaper route. We have done a door-to-door visit to all the houses on her round, but nobody's seen or heard anything useful. So far it is all a blank, I'm afraid.

Whoever shouted to send for Rudi is something to think about actually. The poor man has had a terrible time lately, losing his wife, our lovely Dr Janet and his baby son, maybe it would be a good idea to send for him if only to take his mind off all his troubles. I'll talk to the super about it. Good idea. Now, if we are all finished, that's it for this morning. You have your jobs to do—go to it!"

He strode to the door, followed by his trusty sergeant, to a smattering of applause. Rudi was really well-liked.

Chapter Five

Kylie gradually recovered consciousness. The drug Rohypnol was in her system and she was feeling relaxed, but a little sick from the effect of the ether. She opened her eyes and tried to focus, but everything was blurred. She could hear music and she felt a slight breeze on her body and a sweet perfumed aroma. She tried to gather her thoughts together, but with little success. She knew she felt really lethargic and knew she was really comfortable and lying on something soft and silky. She gave up the effort and went back to sleep, sighing contentedly.

Rohypnol has the effect of relaxing the senses, it is used to spike drinks and facilitate sexual encounters. Often called 'easy lay' for obvious reasons. It works best in combination with alcohol which also is a drug used to counter, in women, the natural resistance to the sexual advances of a hopeful male.

Simon, as said, had no such plans. It was not part of his grand vision at all. She was a child and Simon was not in any way shape or form a paedophile. He, in fact, found children rather a nuisance. Noisy and demanding. Simon was, in fact, still a virgin at the age of thirty. He had no urge to have sex with anyone at all. He was more in love with himself than anyone else, with the sole exception of his adored mother.

He often used his amazing mirrored ballroom so he could look at his own beautiful (in his estimation) nude body from every angle. He also liked to dress up in shiny sexy clothing, such as ballet tights and parade in front of the mirrors admiring his image. His mother often joined in. As noted earlier, they both were naturists at heart. and spent a lot of their time naked. They spent most of their leisure time nakedly happy together. They loved to anoint each other with aromatic oils.

This room was also where they practised their ballet, with their ballet master, who had been employed by the Shaw family for many years and was a close friend. Their favourite ballet was Stravinsky's 'The Rite of Spring' rather oddly, considering its' rampant sexual themes. A psychoanalyst would have been intrigued.

Simon was a total narcissist, so no danger to young Kylie in a sexual way at all. He did not want to defile his holy, cherished and perfect body. Sex was such a messy business, he imagined. In his mind, it was—Ugh, Really? Is that what you do? God! No! His love was on a much higher plane, he imagined and his adoring mother agreed.

Kylie was left to sleep undisturbed on her luxurious couch. Simon would not give her any more injections. He wanted her to return to her senses now, so that he could start on his grand plan, based on one word, **Persuasion**. He needed to persuade the child to voluntarily leave her old life behind and join him in a new life together, as his fairy-tale princess. Cinderella-like, but as a daughter, not a lover.

Ultimately to become a necessary adoring female replacement, in his twisted mind, for his mother, in all the years ahead, which he had lost. If Kylie did not respond how he wanted, after a decent interval, he would destroy her, replace her and keep looking. Only perfection would do.

Chapter Six

Simon Shaw worked in two hospitals. Most of his time was spent in a private hospital, one of a large national group, where he was a consultant plastic surgeon. He also worked in an NHS teaching hospital, like others in his profession. He was universally popular with all the staff, with his good looks, friendly manner and charming personality, leading to him having many devoted fans, especially among the ladies of a certain age.

He was, understandably in great demand for his services, but he seemed to be untiring, always amiable and never impatient or grumpy. Life was good, it seemed, but then Covid-19 intervened.

Simon had taken a year's sabbatical, in order to properly start his grand plan. He now had his first trial all in hand, having abducted Kylie Ellis. He spent most of the first night sitting beside her and monitoring her progress as she slept in her drugged state. Now, he was waiting for her to wake up so that he could make a start on his plan of persuading her to leave her parents and friends and agree to voluntarily become his ward.

Simon knew it would not be easy to persuade the girl the way he wanted and knew it would take all his charm and inducements for him to succeed. He also knew his plan might fail and the girl would persistently refuse all his offers. In that case, he would have no choice but to kill her and somehow dispose of her body. He had not quite worked out a plan for that as yet…

Kylie slept on peacefully enough through the early part of the night—but then her condition started to change. Kylie's face had gone bright pink and she had started to sweat profusely. Her breathing became shallow, laboured and rasping. What Simon did not know was that Kylie was a severe asthmatic—and she had left her inhaler at home, rather than in her satchel, by mistake.

Normally, while at school if she had an attack she was able to control it by using her inhaler. Simon, of course, had looked through the contents of her satchel but had not found the inhaler, which might have alerted him to her condition. He began to be seriously concerned. *Is it Covid-19?* he worried. He knew the girl was really ill and that she needed immediate medical attention because of her breathing problem.

As a surgeon, such a condition was well outside of his experience. She needed to go to hospital, see a physician and be put on oxygen, at the very least. She could also be very infectious! Simon began to panic. He ran out of the room and back to his house, where he flung himself on a chair, trembling with agitation.

He took his own temperature and gasped when it revealed it was over normal. His chest felt tight and he knew he might be having a panic attack, but it did not help. He was furious with the girl—it was all her fault!

He knew he had to get rid of the girl, but did not want to touch her as she probably was highly infectious. He had to get some proper viral protective clothing and he knew, of course, where it was all kept at the hospital where he worked. He rushed out of the house and got into his Jaguar car and roared away. He felt sick with worry.

Chapter Seven

DI Mike Carter and his boss, DCS Len Rowles, were meeting in Len's office, over several cups of excellent coffee from the super's personal coffee-maker machine. It was a routine morning report from the DI. They were good friends as well as colleagues and the chat was cordial and relaxed. Mike was sensible enough not to attempt his habitual witty comments with his boss, as he knew Len would not appreciate it one bit.

The super, despite his massive stature, huge red nose and bald head, was a serious and sensitive soul, a man who loved his work and was not only an excellent detective, he was also an avid criminologist with a wonderful knowledge of criminal behaviour culled largely from his vast collection of books on the subject.

Pride of place in his library were the books on criminal profiling written by his good friend and former colleague, Dr Rudolph Valentine, American FBI Profiler, an authority and lecturer on the subject. Eventually, the conversation had turned to be about Rudi, as he liked to be called.

The super was nearly in tears. He said, "I tell you honestly, Mike, it was the most awful tragedy you could imagine. Rudi's wife and baby both killed outright. I hate to think about it. Such a lovely couple, with everything to live for. It just doesn't seem right. Not right at all, Mike, I tell you—" He had to stop.

Mike said, "I know, Len. Everybody who met Rudi or Janet loved them to bits They were just meant for each other. As I understand it, it was just Janet and baby in the car. She skidded on a muddy track and went into a tree. Is that right, Len?"

"That's right, Mike. Jan was driving on a track through the woods. There had been a torrential storm and she was taking a shortcut back to their ranch after meeting with friends. No other vehicle was involved. It just burst into flames. They had no chance. It was God-awful. Awful!"

Len, who had no close relatives and had never married or been involved with any woman in his life, had loved Rudi like a brother and had been also very fond of Dr Janet McBride who had been the local forensic pathologist for the station. The two had met when Rudi had come over on loan from the FBI to assist the team hunting a serial killer who called himself The Angel of Death nearly two years since.

Mike said, "You have been over to stay with Rudi and his family two or three times since they went back to America, haven't you Len? You've told me what a great life they had over there, on their ranch and suchlike."

"Oh Mike, you have no idea. Their lifestyle was marvellous. Those two were so happy together, it was lovely to see. And then that baby son of theirs was born, Alistair, they called him. Such a bonnie wee lad, as Janet would say, being Scottish by birth. Such a great couple. Rudi is devastated, of course he is, poor man. He'll never get over it—never. Neither will I."

Len was shaking his huge totally bald head, close to tears, his red misshapen nose damply quivering with suppressed emotion. He had never really gotten over losing his older sister who had committed suicide, aged sixteen, after years of being sexually abused by their father. Len had spent years, as a youth, in a mental institution, being treated for consequent manic depression. He had tried and failed to kill his father. That frustrated rage was still buried deep inside him.

Len calmed down. The two men were silent for a minute or two, each occupied with their own thoughts. Len eventually said, very quietly, "You know the old saying: 'to know great sorrow, you must have known great joy'?—how true in this case, Mike."

Mike nodded his agreement, then added, "Look—Len—I don't know whether to say this or not, but here goes anyway. How do you feel about inviting him back over here, for a holiday? We haven't got a serial killer to catch I know, but could he not just come over the visit us and stay with you again, I know how much he liked and admired you and loved your company—and your five cats!

You two got on famously and it would give him a break a long way away from where all his troubles took place. Something different, something to take his mind off his losses. He'll have to make a new life for himself somehow, sometime. What do you think sir?"

Len's eyes glistened. He said, "That's a great idea, Mike. I'd love to see Rudi and have him to stay with me for a while. Nothing would give me greater pleasure, but I don't know, he's surrounded by the love of his family over there. But what you say about him getting away from it all makes sense, I suppose. I'll certainly give it some thought."

He paused for a beat, squared his shoulders and then said, with a smile, "Anyway, we'd better get on with your report Mike. Anything else of interest Detective Inspector?" His forced brightness was touching to see.

"Actually, yes sir, there is. We've got a missing schoolgirl and it has some really worrying aspects to it. Not the usual misper case. It's a twelve-year-old girl called Kylie Thomas, who appears to have been abducted while she was doing her paper round. Her bicycle and paper bag are also missing.

She must have been put in a van or a large car, together with her bike and the papers and taken off somewhere for purposes unknown. She is nearly thirteen and is described, by her mother, as being well-developed and very pretty. I have got a really nasty feeling about this, sir."

"I presume the usual procedures have been followed, without any success?"

"Indeed, sir. All the usual searches, including fingertip searches of the lane where she must have been taken. All the enquiries have been made, all with nothing to show for it at all. There is no possibility, of course, that this is a kidnap case. Kylie's parents have no money to spare. They rent their house and have no capital to speak of, sir."

"OK, Detective Inspector. Thank you for your excellent report, as usual—I'll see you tomorrow. We can only hope that in the case of this missing girl, Kylie, you say? something will turn up soon. Keep me informed, of course."

At that moment there was a loud rap on the office door.

"Come!" said the superintendent.

It was Detective Sergeant Phipps. He looked excited, which for him, was most unusual.

"Yes, Sergeant?"

"Arr, Has the Inspector told yow about the missing schoolgirl, Kylie Thomas, sir?"

"Yes, he has. You have some news about this case, Phippy?"

"Arr I 'ave, sir She's been found, dead, lying by her bicycle and the papers. In the lane, she was taken from, loike, sir." (Phippy was trying to 'spake proper' for the super, but it was a struggle!)

"What?" The superintendent's massive frame half-lifted from his vast chair.

"Crikey Moses!" added DI Mike.

"Arr, sirs." (Phippy's deeply-lined doleful face was returning to normal). "The poor kiddie's body was discovered early this morning by another young girl delivering newspapers, would yow believe. A friend of Kylie's as well. Must have been a dreadful shock for the poor youngster. She's with a counsellor.

Kylie had been missing exactly two whole days. The forensics are theer now, with Kim, our pathologist. She should be reporting in soon, but as far as she can tell, so far, the girl seems to have doyd from natural causes, loike. Oh and she ain't been interfered with or harmed in any way as far as the doc can see at this toime, loike, sirs."

"What?" repeated the super, this time rising all the way onto his feet and presenting an awesome sight. His huge bald head and quivering red nose seemingly filling all the office space.

Phippy backed off a pace. "Er, that's all I know at this moment sirs."

"Where exactly is this scene of crime, Phippy?" asked Mike.

Phippy described the lane from where the girl had been abducted and was now returned.

The two senior detectives headed for the door and the car park. As a parting thrust Len shouted, to the sergeant, "Contact the SOC team at once and tell them not to move the body 'til we get there! You take over as Crime Scene Manager sergeant."

"Royt y'ar sirs!" said Phippy, getting out his mobile phone. He intended to return to the scene of crime himself. He would take charge as Crime Scene Manager with pleasure.

Chapter Eight

Dr Prof. Simon Shaw sat in his house scowling at the view outside. All his carefully-laid plans were in tatters. He was back to square one. Also, he was terrified of being discovered as a child abductor. He knew he had made rash decisions, forced on him by circumstances he could not have anticipated. He had had to go and get some viral protective clothes from the private hospital where he worked as a consultant cosmetic surgeon.

He had arrived in the middle of the night, had rushed in and grabbed the masks and clothes from a cupboard, stuffed them in his briefcase and rushed out again. Someone must have seen him, he thought, grimly. But he had not seen anyone take any notice of him, so he hoped he had gotten away with it.

After donning the protective clothing he had gone out to check on the girl. Rather to his expectation, she had died. His first thought was that she was probably not infectious now, as she wasn't breathing, so that was a relief. He had grabbed her body and ran out to his white van, he then went back and collected the girl's bike and her paper round bag.

He had driven carefully and slowly back to the lane from where he had done the abduction and unceremoniously dumped the girl, her bike and her bag on the verge somewhere near to where he had done the deed, two days before. He had gotten back in his van and driven home. Again, slowly and quietly. He knew that roaring along the roads at night would alert some nosy parker looking out of his or her window.

He knew that if he left no trace, he could never be arrested for the crime. He hoped he had done his best, in very trying circumstances. That blasted child! Why the hell—? He drew some comfort from blaming poor Kylie for his current dilemma. But he knew he had a good chance of catching Covid-19 from her—that blasted horrible child! He felt ill.

He took his temperature again. It had gone up further. He fell asleep in his chair, exhausted.

The next day he felt worse. His temperature was now so high he knew he had a fever. He started to cough and cough and could not find relief. He was terrified. He struggled to breathe. He was in a complete panic. In desperation, he rang 999 for an ambulance. It seemed to take an age to arrive and he had an awful time trying to grant them access through his gates and into his house.

He was in a state of collapse and only kept going by a supreme effort of will. He thought he was dying. When the ambulance staff found him he was semi-conscious on the floor and blue in the face. It was touch and go. The ambulance staff put him on oxygen and gave him a jab of adrenaline, plus a saline drip, then rushed him off to the A&E of the NHS hospital where he also worked as a consultant. He was immediately put on a ventilator. The doctors present shook their heads sadly.

But Simon was young, fit and strong and he made a remarkable recovery, though he remained in hospital for some weeks. Of course, the media had a field day! They gave full rein in their most purple prose to tell the adoring public about the brave young and handsome consultant who had risked his life for his patients and had succumbed to the dread virus. All total nonsense, Simon had never gone near the Covid-19 wards having avoided them literally like a plague. But the media are never going to let the truth mar a good story—Simon was a hero!

In the following weeks, naturally enough, the story faded away, but then Simon returned home, after running the gauntlet of all the staff of the hospital apartment who had saved his life, through all the happy smiles and congratulations and applause, reported on the local TV and papers. Another brief moment of glory, which he modestly acknowledged as his due.

The security firm which looked after his house had done a good job. No one had managed to gain access through his gates. The electronics had worked well.

So Simon was back home and continuing to work on his Grand Plan. He had gotten over his disappointment about the first girl he had abducted and did not blame himself one bit. That was just an unfortunate blip and not his fault. She would have been an excellent choice, it was just a bit of bad luck that she had contacted Covid-19 and was an asthmatic. How was he to have known that?

Kylie was good, but surely he could do better next time. While in his hospital bed he noticed the pretty young blonde-haired nurse who had attended to his needs. He smiled at her in a calculating way and asked her to tell him about herself. Of course, she was delighted. What a catch! She stuck out her breasts and dreamed of marriage!

In fact, Simon wondered if Kylie had been too young for his purpose. Next time, he determined, he would go for someone a bit older. But the nurse was probably too old, really. No, not the nurse. Oh well. He looked forward to his quest for a replacement for Kylie. Next time there would be no mistakes!

Chapter Nine

The Detective Inspector and his boss, the superintendent, had arrived at the familiar scene, similar to so many in the past. The flashing lights, the police and ambulance vehicles, the tents, the miles of blue and white striped plastic tape, stating "Police, do not cross" time and time again.

The uniform officers were busy, doing a finger-tip search along the lane and verges. The crime scene bods were taking measurements, photographs, recording everything in sight.

Mike and Len went straight to the tent erected around the body of the child victim. Inside they found forensic pathologist, Dr Kim Masters, still examining Kylie's pathetic little corpse. The doc looked around at the two men, the massive bulk of the super dwarfing his companions and making the tent seem tiny.

She said, with a wry smile, "Sometimes I hate this job," and added, "but I'm glad to see you both, Len, Mike, I'll move outside and give you a bit more room to have a look at the poor child."

The two men nodded their heads in acknowledgement, as they greeted Kim warmly. Everybody liked Kim, a tall, rangy lady, married with two small children, brilliant at her chosen career, with a generally pleasant face, now clouded with distaste at her awful task. Everyone hated having to deal with dead children, from whatever cause, with child murder being fortunately very rare.

Kylie lay on her side. The pathologist had unfastened the girl's bright pink coat but otherwise had left exactly as she had found her. A police doctor had earlier just to confirm death had taken place. Scene of crime officers had removed Kylie's pink bicycle but had carefully marked and labelled the spot where it been found.

Len said, "Christ, Mike—our living nightmare, a murdered child. She looks as if she is asleep, the poor kid. She is beautiful. How can anyone, however evil, do this?" His voice was husky and his face was running with tears. Mike's eyes were watering too. He felt sick.

Dead bodies always give off a horrible smell, a smell never forgotten once experienced and lingering in the mind for hours despite all attempts to blot it out. Somehow the school uniform made the sight quite unbearable. Obscene. Mike's own little girl had just had her first school uniform and he had proudly taken her photograph wearing it only yesterday. How cute she looked!

The two policemen came out of the tent, mopping their eyes, rather to the surprise of Kim, who had never before seen hardened police officers like these showing such emotion.

Len was shaking his huge bald head in sorrow. "Christ!" he said again, this time with a savage growl. Mike looked pale and shaken. He was thinking about having to tell Kylie's mum and dad and getting one of them to identify the body. He did not know whether he could face it.

Len said, "Sorry about that, Kim. Look, what can you tell us?" He could not look her in the eye.

Kim said, warmly, "Don't worry, Len, it is lovely to see you so emotional about this poor little girl and you too, Mike. It truly is enough to make the most hardened veteran cop shed a tear—and rightly so. But, you know, I really don't think this child has been harmed by whoever was holding her. I think I can say that she died of natural causes, asthma attack, lack of oxygen, possibly Covid-19 at a guess.

Obviously, I will need to do a pm on the girl to be sure, but that's how it looks to me at present. So, I think the perpetrator did not kill her, there is really no sign of violence at all. He took her, she fell ill and died, so he brought her back here.

On the other hand, he should have called an ambulance when she fell ill, so he is responsible in that way, but he probably thought he could not do that without giving himself away. It's an abduction that went wrong, tragically, I reckon guys. Whatever that perp wanted to do with the girl, I dread to think, but I don't think he intended just to kill her."

Mike said, "Thanks, Kim. Brilliant as ever. For a pathologist, you're the best detective on the force, mate."

Kim coloured slightly at the handsome young inspector's flattery but said nothing in reply. She knew she was overstepping her role in what she had said, but did not really care. She gives her opinion. That's the way she is. Like it or lump it. She wondered, though, if Mike was gently ticking her off in a roundabout way, saying, in effect, leave the detecting to the detectives. Men! She went back into the tent, nodding a rather icy goodbye.

Len said, quietly, "Come on Mike, we're only in the way here, but I did want to see for myself. I see Phippy's now in charge, so that's fine. There's no one better."

The pair walked back to their car. Len suggested they find a café and have a coffee break. There was a Costa outlet not too far away and they headed for that. The coffee was not bad there and they did some really good toasties—ham and cheese a favourite for both the men.

When they were settled at a table, which seemed far too small for the massive superintendent and the detective inspector, who was no wimp himself—although of middling height he had a very muscular body, with a big chest and broad shoulders plus an enviable flat stomach. Mike was a target for the young ladies at the station, despite the fact that they knew he was a devoted family man with a gorgeous wife and two beautiful children. But they could dream on.

It was his thick, wavy black hair and finely-shaped hands and his glow of health that made him quite irresistible. But only a mother could fancy the super perhaps—though it was a known fact that some gorillas in zoos were often gazed at longingly by adoring females—human as well as ape!

Of course, they discussed the case they had just been to see, quietly, almost in whispers, while they were waiting for their toasties to be brought to them. A sort of deep rumble from the super, that had Mike straining his ears to interpret. It was made worse when the toasties arrived, which both men wolfed down in seconds.

"So, Mike, what were your first impressions?"

"Well, Len, I confess to being completely baffled by this one. It is the motive that seems to me to be the main problem here. Why would anyone want to abduct a young and pretty schoolgirl and then, without interfering with her sexually, just return her to the spot where she was taken? It is beyond me."

"Mm," agreed the super. "That's about the size of it, Mike. Kim is probably right when she suggests the girl was suffering from a serious illness and being abducted brought on an attack of asthma or something that killed her. We must find out from her doctor whether she *was* asthmatic of course and if so, wouldn't she have had an inhaler thing for that? I can see the dilemma that the perpetrator might well have found himself in.

If Kim is right and the girl was ill, maybe dying, with Covid-19 as well as an asthma attack, he might well have panicked and behaved in the way we have just witnessed. I have great faith in Kim—you're right Mike—for a pathologist, she has a damned fine detective brain. She's quite a treasure.

Agreed. But let's consider what our perp wanted to do the girl. The motive. I mean the usual motivation in an abduction is to gain a load of money or for sexual gratification—or trafficking perhaps. None of those can be eliminated so far, although extortion of money seems a forlorn hope as her family is not rich.

I think it was simply a paedophile looking for a young girl, maybe to sell on to a paedo ring or for his own amusement and then, as is usual, to kill her and dispose of the body somehow. However, I rather think if the girl *had* died of natural causes, he would still make use of her body, so that might be ruled out. As I say, Len, it is beyond me!"

Len said nothing for a while, just drained his coffee, grabbed the paper napkin and wiped his generous mouth.

Eventually, he said, "I look forward to your report tomorrow, Mike. God knows where we go with this one though. We'd better get back and get weaving. Team meeting 10 am. I *will* be attending."

53

Chapter Ten

Kylie's mum, Carol, was dishing up her husband's evening meal when the doorbell rang. Ronnie called out, "OK. love, I'll go!" and went out to open the door.

On the doorstep stood DI Mike Carter and DC Penny Summers, holding out their IDs, even though they had both been to the house before, especially Penny, but it was the first time either of them had met Ronnie, who worked long hours at his job as a self-employed painter and decorator.

Ronnie went pale as he saw the looks on the faces of the two coppers. He swayed forwards and Mike lunged at him, grabbing him by the arm. To say that Kylie had been the apple of her dad's eye would vastly underrate the love he had for his only child. And Kylie worshipped her dad. He was her hero. A small, thin, wiry man with a beard and a nice smiley face, always laughing and joking, he was very popular with all his friends, acquaintances and customers alike.

He led the coppers into the front parlour of the house and asked them to sit down. Carol rushed in, wiping her hands, her face strained and drawn.

She said, "Well?" loudly, desperately. She knew right away.

Mike looked at Penny despairingly, he seemed unable to speak. Penny got to her feet and said, quietly, "I cannot say how sorry we are, but we have found a body and we are sure it is Kylie, Mr and Mrs Thomas. It is what we have all been dreading." Carol rushed out of the room but turned on her heel and rushed back again.

"I knew it! I knew it! I knew she was dead! A mother knows, she knows, she knows." Her voice tailed away and she dropped into a chair and wailed like a lost soul in hell. "My poor little girl, dead!"

Ronnie kneeled in front of her and she clasped him to her, both of them absolutely bereft with grief. Then Ronnie tore himself away and rushed out of the room, noises from the downstairs toilet told of him being violently sick. Carol rushed out of the room too.

Mike and Penny just stared dumbly at each other. They now had to ask one of the Thomas's to come with them to formally identify the body. Several minutes rolled by. Eventually, Ronnie, white of face, came and joined them.

"I'm sorry," he muttered.

Then Carol appeared. She screamed, "Was she interfered with? Tell me, I want to know!"

Mike assured her that her daughter had not been harmed in any way, that she had died of natural causes as far as the doctors could tell.

This shocked the parents completely. For a moment neither of them spoke. Then Ronnie blurted, "B-but, there was nothing wrong with her, apart from her asthma and that was under control." Then he quavered, trembling violently, "Oh my God! She left her puffer here, she left it in her school satchel. She always took it with her on her paper round, because she went straight on to the school after finishing her round, but that day she must have forgotten to take it with her. It's still here, hanging on her peg in the hallway."

Carol said, very loudly, "I want to see her. I want to see her, NOW!" She was glaring at Mike and standing close to him belligerently, arms akimbo.

Penny breathed a sigh of relief. She said, "Of course—we need you to confirm her identity anyway, so we want to take both of you with us to the mortuary, as soon as you are ready."

Ronnie said, hesitantly, "I don't think—"

Carol butted in, "No, Ronnie, love, you stay here." She turned to the two coppers and said, "He couldn't cope, the poor man." She suddenly appeared strong and calm. She grabbed a coat from a peg in the hallway and walked out of the door towards the police car.

It was a short drive to the mortuary. They piled out of the car and were duly admitted into the building. They had to wait, while the staff got ready for them and then they were shown into the corridor, where through a window they could see a body covered with a white sheet, with an attendant at its head.

The member of staff pulled back the sheet to show the child's head. Apart from her blue colour, she looked peaceful and asleep. It seemed to Carol impossible that she was lying there dead. She turned to Penny, her eyes wild with grief, "What's wrong with her? Yes, of course, that's my Kylie, my baby. Why is she so still? She looks cold. You must warm her up, she needs some blankets and a hot water bottle then she'll be fine."

Her eyes rolled in her head and Mike and Penny had to grab her as she fell unconscious into their arms.

Chapter Eleven

Birmingham Airport, a vast and impressive building, was strangely quiet. The Covid-19 pandemic had caused travelling numbers to plummet. Superintendent Len Rowles was standing in the Arrivals area, waiting for the plane from the USA to arrive, one of only three planes that day.

Dr Prof. Rudolph Valentine had managed to get a visa to travel to England on a 'Working Holiday'—which was stretching the truth a little—but he would have to go into a 10-day isolation on his arrival, spending this period at the home of his host, where he had stayed the last time he had come to help the detective team. The plane was due in at noon, UK time, which would be some five hours ahead of the time that Rudi had left the States, late the previous evening.

Rudi was well used to jet travel, he had done it all his working career at very frequent intervals, mainly in his own vast country, as an eminent psychologist and FBI Profiler. He was also a world authority on serial murders, having been among the team that developed the FBI Profiling System itself over the years.

Despite many disbelievers, the system had really helped to catch some of the USA's worst serial offenders, such as the notorious Unabomber, who had terrorised the population for years, by sending bombs through the post to people he felt should be eliminated for damaging the ecology of the planet.

Len had no trouble recognising his friend, despite him wearing a mask, when he arrived through the gates, although he was shocked by the strain he saw in his familiar, very handsome, face. He looked somewhat older than the last time he had met him, as a guest in the American's ranch, with his adored wife and wee bairn—his wife being a Scottish lady they sometimes used Scottish terms, which delighted their American friends and family equally.

Len and Rudi had become close friends when Rudi had stayed with Len and his five cats in his Birmingham suburban home. Rudi had come over to assist Len's team in the case of the so-called "Angel of Death"—the serial killer preying on comfortably-off elderly men in the Wolverhampton area, strangling his victims and hammering a wooden stake into their chests.

During his visit, Rudi had met and fallen in love with the forensic pathologist working on the same case and he had taken her back with him to the States and married her. They had had a baby son and life had been good until the awful accident in which both Rudi's wife and son had died. Len was so looking forward to having Rudi as his guest for a holiday, hopefully to start healing some wounds while over here.

The two masked men met in the strangely formal way dictated by Covid-19 restrictions, just touching elbows as approved at the time. In any case, Len hated being touched— a hangover from his childhood when his older sister had been sexually abused by their father, leading to the young girl's suicide and Len needing years of mental care in hospital.

But the greetings from both men were bright and cheerful and the ice was soon broken. Rudi was such a charmer and this was still very much in evidence, despite his continuing grief for his wife and baby son.

In a very short period of time, Len's car was loaded with Rudi's small amount of luggage and the two men set off for Len's home, in the rather upmarket town of Solihull, where many of the more executive types working in Birmingham had their homes.

When they arrived, they were greeted by Len's five cats, named Number One, Two, Three, Four and Five—all British Blues and identical to a casual observer, but Len knew who was who, and Rudi still remembered how to identify the differences. Like last time, he was soon on his back, covered by cats, licking him affectionately. Their meowing was quite a cats' cacophony of sounds!

From that very time, Rudi felt the healing process had started if just a little. As an eminent psychologist, he knew of the healing power of the love of animals very well and the many pets he had back at his ranch in Florida had been a huge source of comfort to him, as well as the support of his family—four sisters and mum and dad, all living in the vast ranch estate grounds.

After his long and tiring journey, despite his first-class accommodation on the plane, all Rudi wanted to do was a have a quick snack, a glass of wine and bed. The two men had carefully kept the conversation light and cheery, with no mention of recent traumatic events.

As Rudi would be confined to the house for ten days he would spend all of the time relaxing, reading, chatting to Len in the evenings and maybe watching some TV. No work, no pressure, just R&R—rest and recuperation. Charging the batteries, so to speak. At Len's, there would be nothing to remind him of his lost wife and child, which was a true blessing.

But after a week of this pleasant routine, a much more relaxed Rudi than the one who arrived at Len's doorstep, said, in a mock upper-class English accent, "Well, my dear Watson, have you any interesting cases on your books at this time, to recount for me, just for a change of topic?"

Len chuckled—a deep rumbling sound—and replied, in keeping with the mood, "'Fraid not, Holmes, old man, no Angel of Death or indeed no serial killers of any kind to amuse you with! Sorry!" His fake accent was, if anything, even worse than his companion's.

They both chuckled and smiled at each other with affection. They had become very close in that last week and Rudi was really very grateful to the massive superintendent, who had been scrupulously careful and really soothing to his tortured and grieving soul—helped by those wonderful and very intelligent family of beautiful cats. When either man was sitting, there was always one of the cats on each of their laps, purring contentedly. The purring had an amazing healing and calming effect.

Rudi continued, no longer as Sherlock, "Look, Len, I know serial killers are quite rare in England, compared to us stateside, but surely there must be one or two interesting cases, which are worth mentioning? Come on, man, surely there must be some good mysteries to solve? After all, some of the most intriguing cases are not murders at all, like kidnap, fraud, assault and the like. I know we had some great conversations about famous crimes of the past last time I was here and even when you were on holiday with us at the ranch, I really feel the need of some crime talk to tickle my fancy, Len. It's my life."

Rudi smiled one of his incredible 1000-watt brilliant smiles that light up the room—for the first time in months. Len was delighted, of course and his own rugged and craggy face also lit up in wide grin, looking like a gigantic mischievous elf.

Len thought for a moment and then said, "Well, if you insist, Rudi—there is one case we have at this time which is both shocking and disturbing and a real puzzler for you. I'm not asking you to assist us, let me make that clear, you are here for a holiday and a break from your usual routine, but as you have made that request, I'll try to outline the case to you."

Rudi's eyes lit up in anticipation. "Tell me!" he said.

"Right! Well, it started out as a simple missing-person case. A pretty young working-class schoolgirl, named Kylie, out delivering newspapers disappeared one early morning. All the usual procedures to find her yielded nothing. It became clear that she had been abducted by a person or persons unknown, for a reason unknown.

Nothing to really get too excited about you might say and you might think, as we did, that the girl was taken by a paedophile for his sexual pleasure. We rather expected that after a few days a body would be found giving evidence of that predictable kind."

Rudi interjected, eagerly, "But something odd happened!"

Len chuckled again and tried to keep the conversation light-hearted, "Indeed it did, my dear Holmes—bend your mighty intellect on this—after only two days the girl was found, back in the exact place from where she had been abducted, with her missing bicycle and the undelivered papers in their bag. She had died of natural causes, probably the result of an asthma attack and the onset of Covid-19 during her captivity, but was otherwise unharmed and not interfered with in any way. So what do you make of that, my dear sir? What? Elementary?"

Rudi chuckled again but then became serious, "Well, Len, as you say, an unusual case. Tell me more."

So Len filled his friend in with all the details he knew of the case. Rudi went very quiet and was lost in thought.

After a while Len, said, quietly, "Come on then Rudi, you can tell me, as a psychologist and an expert of human criminal behaviour, what do your thinking may have happened here?"

Rudi looked grave. "I think you may have a real problem with this one, Len. I don't like the sound of it one bit. It could turn out to be ten times worse than your Angel of Death case, which was, in essence, straightforward revenge murder. I am really worried, old friend. Whoever is responsible for this crime, is, in my opinion, a terrible danger to other young girls. He needs to be stopped, at all costs. He really does. This is just the start!"

Part Two
Natalie

Chapter One

Rollingberg High School, one of the top exclusive academies for girls in the Midlands, was in full swing. The recent lockdowns had ended and the students were happy to be back to something like normal. Being back among their friends was the best part, for the girls, of course.

Down a corridor, floor gleaming, walking, talking, giggling, were three of the students, all close friends, Natalie, Julie and Kathy. They were on their way to the dinner hall and being young and healthy, they had good appetites and were looking forward to their lunch.

Natalie was tall, blonde and willowy, while both Julie and Kathy were small and a bit on the plump side, puppy fat maybe. Natalie was a natural leader and what Natalie wanted was generally what happened, but Kathy had the best brain, being one of the top students in the school for academic achievements, she was a bit shy and quiet, but strong-willed nevertheless.

Once Kathy had made up her mind, there was no budging her. Julie was funny, the school comic, always joking and larking about, loving to impersonate the teachers, making her friends howl with laughter. Julie was also the most active of the three friends, always on the go, bright and bubbly as a robin. All three were very close. They had made a solemn pact that they would not bother with boys, rather to be satisfied just with the company of each other.

They were fourteen years old and their hormones were jumping about wildly, causing mood swings, tantrums and angst. Not an easy time for them.

Of course, parents and in particular, mothers, were a standard topic of conversation. Rarely complimentary.

Julie gabbled, "Honestly! My mother! She is the very limit. She sits there at home all day long watching TV shopping channels or leafing through clothes catalogues— and if she is not doing that she's at a coffee morning" (she made a face) "or something equally dumb headed—then she has the nerve to tell me *I'm* not working hard enough. I *mean!*"

Natalie drawled, raising her rather beautiful big blue eyes heavenwards, "Huh—tell me about it." Then they all giggled helplessly, hugging each other.

All three girls were wearing tee-shirts and tiny pelmets of skirts, showing off nearly all of their legs up to the swell of their plump buttocks. The tee-shirts were displaying American-type college graphics. Julie's for example, bearing the number 49 in white against a bright green background.

Natalie's long, slim, shapely legs were the envy of most the school's girls, many of them having legs rather like tree trunks, sadly.

Of course, all three friends wore short white socks and the latest trendy trainers. They were all in the school 'cheerleaders' group, another US import, like also the much-anticipated 'Prom' when they reached the giddy-height of being 'Leavers'. They couldn't wait to be older!

Dr Simon Shaw was chairman of the governors of the school, taking over from his mother, who had held the post for some years. As a local celebrity, she had attracted the local monied families and had been a regular donor to the school herself and had paid for two extensions, including a concert hall/theatre that was a focus for many talented young musicians, dancers and actors, giving the school a huge cultural reputation.

Now, Simon was carrying on where she left off and was very much admired and respected himself, as a musician and particularly as a guest conductor of the school orchestra. Simon was also an advisor to the school music department, which was an important part of the school's cultural compass. All the students and most of the staff simply adored the young man, almost as much as he adored himself.

As occasional conductor of the school orchestra, he had noticed young Natalie, who played the oboe to quite a good standard for her age and experience. As with everything she did, she showed great enthusiasm and dedication which Simon greatly admired. However, she did not share the almost universal love displayed by the other girls, many of whom had a huge crush on the handsome doctor.

She thought he was a conceited and patronising bore and did not like him at all. The only boys to catch her attention tended to be very laid back and 'cool' the sort who rebelled against something or other and looked rather untidy and unruly, with wild hair and shirts hanging out of their shabby trousers. Not that there were any boys at the school in any event! She just saw the lads drifting down the roads kicking balls and larking about like they do.

The Covid-19 pandemic had put an end to the orchestra of course and the concert hall had had no rehearsals or performances since the lockdown and was only just beginning to think of restarting, as the government started to relax some of the restrictions. The closure, though, presented an opportunity for Simon, as an advisor and conductor of the orchestra, he had access to the girl by letter or telephone and under lockdown, he imagined Natalie would jump at the chance to have some private tutorials on her oboe, with a professional.

His big idea was to pretend to be a member of the Birmingham Symphony Orchestra, the lead oboist to be exact—he thought he might entice Natalie to come to a false private tuition session which would give him an opportunity of abducting her. He concocted a story that, as the BSO was currently unable to play concerts, some of the individual professional musicians would be volunteering their services to school orchestra members, giving what might be called masterclasses.

Using school notepaper, he sent a letter to Natalie detailing the offer of some individual oboe masterclass sessions, signing them in a fictitious name. After much thought, he came up with the name Anna Czyszwk, a made-up Polish-sounding name, very difficult to pronounce for an English speaker.

He thought this would deter her from making enquiries about the offer. It also sounded rather impressive, he imagined, to the youngster! He had signed the letter simply, 'Anna' printing the false full name beneath. The venue was to be the school music department, the time 8 pm in the evening. He banked on the girl coming on her bicycle, as he had found out that she always came to school on her bike. It would be dark, there would be only him there, waiting by the school gates.

As she came through he would abduct her, in the same way as he had taken Kylie, which he proudly thought had worked perfectly. As Chair of the Governors, he knew the necessary codes to open the gates. Simon's letter insisted that the girl bring his letter with her to the school. If he saw a problem, he would simply abort. He went to prepare his little white van, his hands trembling with excitement.

Chapter Two

Natalie was in her bedroom at home, doing some schoolwork, when a knock came at her door.

"Who is it?" she called, although she knew full well it must be her big sister, Melissa. The two girls had an uneasy relationship these days, as Melissa was a rather bossy person, as big sisters often are. Now that Natalie was fourteen she considered herself an adult and so she should be able to do what she liked. Melissa was no longer a teenager, she was a grown woman of twenty! A gap of six years was huge at this age.

Also, Melissa was not quite as pretty as her sister. She was a little overweight, as she loved cakes. She was envious of Natalie's good looks, her clear skin and long shiny hair and especially her long legs and slim body. She hated how their father obviously was proud of and obsessed with his youngest daughter and rather dismissive of his firstborn, with whom he appeared rather disappointed.

However, Melissa had done well academically at school and now a student in the third year of a medical degree in physiotherapy at Birmingham University, where she shared a flat with three other girls. She was not at home too often these days, coming every few weeks or so, usually with a pile of dirty washing for her long-suffering mother to launder.

The two youngsters' mother, Jessica Ellis, ran a Horse Rescue Stables, at the end of their road. It was a registered charity and gave riding lessons to disabled children and worked with local schools and hostels. The two sisters both loved horses and spent a lot of their time at the stables, helping out.

When Melissa got her degree, later this year, she hoped to find employment in the NHS sector. She was friendly and chatty and good with the public, so she thought she had a good chance of making a pleasant career for herself, as a qualified nurse, both in this country and abroad. She loved to travel and saw this career as a good opportunity to see the world. She had already contacted her local hospital trust and had received an encouraging response. She would spend a few years locally gaining experience and then—the world would be her oyster!

Natalie wanted to be a vet. She fancied the young handsome long-haired vet who came to her mother's stables to see to the horses' health. She thought he was gorgeous! He also was in a local amateur rock band! Wow!

Of course, he was flattered by the young girl's attention and he gave her encouragement to think of making her career in veterinary medicine. He had often talked to her about his own career and offered her good advice and information, much to her delight. Now that vets could call themselves 'doctor', she dreamed of being Dr Natalie Ellis one glorious day in the future! Or maybe a rock chick, with black lipstick and white make-up. Or—

So when the door opened and her big sister came in, Natalie gave her a great big smile and said, "Hi there, Mel, what's new?"

"Nothing. I've made a cuppa and I wondered if you wanted one." She was carrying a loaded tray.

"Sure thing. Thanks, Mel, yes please."

Natalie did the honours with the teapot, after pouring some milk in two mugs decorated with pictures of cute kittens. There were some fancy biscuits on a plate so she helped herself to one. Melissa, who was on a diet, did not take one, though she longed to do so. It was just after 11 am.

The two girls jumped on the bed beside each other, as it was a five-foot bed, necessary for when friends came for a sleepover.

"So you're off back to uni this morning, then?" asked Natalie.

"Yes, I'm driving back there in a few minutes, so I thought I'd have a quick chat with you before I go. I've said my bye-byes to Daddy and Mum before she left to go to her stables this morning. That's the trouble with horses, they need such a lot of looking after—every blessed day—it's a good job we've got such a lot of kids volunteering to help out with them, isn't it?"

"Mm, that's right," mumbled Natalie while chewing a Jaffa Cake biscuit.

"What are you doing—no school today?"

"Nope! It's a free study day, something to do with the pandemic. But I must tell you, Mel, tonight, at 8 o'clock, I'm going for a masterclass on my oboe, with a Polish lady who is Principal Oboe for the BSO. Her name's Anna something—I can't pronounce her surname. Apparently, some of the musicians of the orchestra are volunteering their services to schools during this period when they can't give concerts and stuff."

"Ooh, you're lucky! Where will you have to go? How will you get there? Is Mum taking you or what?"

"Oh no, it's at school. I'm going on my bike, as usual. Mum's quite happy, she had a letter from the school, so it's all above board, no prob."

"Well, you be careful. It will be dark and there are some nasty people around. Go straight there, as fast as you can and come straight back again!"

Natalie pouted. "There you go! Treating me like a child. I'm fourteen you know—I can take care of myself!"

"Maybe you can, but be careful, anyway. I have to go now, it's a horrible drive to Birmingham and I want to get out before the traffic gets impossible. So, anyway, I'll see you when I get back. Have a nice time—and help Mum, she's not as young as she used to be, you know."

"All right, all right, I know, I know, don't go on *big sister*. I hope your studies go well. You have a great time. Bye, love you." She gave her big sister a hug and a peck on the cheek, nearly spilling both mugs of tea in the process. She always was clumsy and accident-prone.

"Love you," said Mel, jumping off the bed and ruffling Natalie's hair, playfully.

Little did Melissa know, she would never see her little sister again.

Chapter Three

Late that afternoon, Natalie sat with her father, David, and her mother, Jessica, finishing off their evening meal. Jessica was tired, no doubt, she had had a difficult day at the stables. The local school had visited in the morning and a group of disabled children had been in the afternoon.

The horses were not behaving themselves very well. They had their ups and their downs and this day it mostly downs. They fretted and stamped their hooves, shook their heads and generally were unsettled. Something had disturbed them, but what it was not easy to determine. Looking after horses is a lot of work and they need constant care and attention. As one of the volunteers said, smiling, 'they are frightened by anything that moves and more so by things that stay still!'

This got a good laugh, but the horses were not amused. It took a lot of time and patience to calm them down and with disabled kids, it was especially stressful. Luckily, though, that day nothing untoward had happened, nobody fell off or was reduced to tears, but it was not a good day and Jessica then had to come home and cook a meal. She was shattered, to say the least.

It did not help that her husband, David, was at his most jovial and noisy self. He was a good-natured man by nature and was seldom cast down, but when he was laughing and telling jokes, in his loud voice, clowning around, it sometimes irritated his wife to distraction—especially so when she was tired. It was a strain trying not to show it. Of course, Natalie, who idolised her dad, was equally in high spirits. Neither she nor her father really noticed Jessica's drawn face and slumped posture.

Jessica said, "So you're off to school tonight to have a lesson on your oboe like that letter said. I know you've missed the school orchestra and your friends and that, so it will be nice for you darling, but I'm not all that happy about you going out by yourself in the dark. I think your dad should go with you on his bike to make sure you get there safe and sound. Give us a ring as soon as you get there, all right?"

Natalie rolled her eyes but nodded her head dutifully.

Her dad added, to his wife, "Well, yes, I'd go with her— but my bike is off the road, I haven't ridden it for ages, as you well know. I did offer to run her there in my car, but she does not want me to—I do trust her to be safe really, she lives on that bike of hers and she's never had any sort of accident. I'm quite sure she'll be fine, won't you sweetheart," he grabbed her arms playfully.

"She's a big girl now, fourteen and a very sensible and grown-up fourteen too. Come on, lovely, we'd better go and wash up the dishes before you go and tidy up a bit, we can't leave everything to your mum! It's nearly seven o'clock now and it takes you ten minutes to cycle to school. You must get there nice and early, now, I always say, 'if you are not five minutes early, you're late!'" He roared with laughter at his feeble joke and his family joined in as expected of them.

So, the chores done, Natalie got herself ready. Her dad got her bike out of the garage for her and the two parents waved her away—never to see her again alive.

Natalie had told them that the masterclass was an hour at most and said she would ring again when she was on her way home.

David and Jessica thought she must have forgotten to ring them when she arrived at the school and assured themselves that the excitement of meeting her friends after such a long time must have driven the thought of ringing them out of her mind. But when no ring came at nine o'clock and then ten past the hour, they became worried. Both parents went out of their house and looked up the road, hoping to see her light as Natalie cycled home. Nothing.

David got his car out and went the short distance to the school gates. All was in darkness. They had tried ringing the school, of course, with no answer. It just kept asking them to leave a message after the tone—

At 10 o'clock Jessica rang the local police station. The girl on the desk was polite, but not very helpful. She said no one was available, but that if their daughter had not returned by the morning, to ring again. Jessica screamed down the telephone to no avail. The receptionist kept calm and repeated endlessly that the police could do nothing until the morning, saying that the station would be open from 6 am.

The distraught parents did not go to bed that night. They walked the streets looking hopelessly for their daughter, then took both their cars out and cruised around, tears running down their faces. Neither parent knew the numbers of Natalie's friends, they were all on the girl's phone and nowhere else. Nor did they know where the friends lived, so they were totally unable to contact anyone.

They knew Natalie went around with a gang of friends and they had often seen them at home and at the stables, but they had never got to know any of them very well. They really had not got a clue where any of them lived and were not even certain of their first names, as they seemed to use nicknames for each other. It was hopeless. In any case, during the lockdown, Natalie had stayed at home and so had her friends, of course.

Simon installed Natalie, drugged and unconscious, into his private leisure centre building, setting her down on the white leather lounger where Kylie had been laid many months ago. His face was wreathed in smiles. It had all gone like clockwork. No problems at all. And this girl was far better than the last one.

This was it! From now on it would be plain sailing! He took her oboe out of its case and tried blowing down it. All he succeeded in producing were some squeaks and fart like sounds, so he collapsed in a fit of maniacal giggles. Then he smashed it up, stamping on it with his feet until he was exhausted.

Chapter Four

The police receptionist had left a note on DC Penny Summers'
desk to the effect that a Mrs Jessica Ellis had reported that her
daughter was missing, timed late last evening. In fact, she
already knew of the incident as both Mrs Ellis and her
husband had been to the station from the moment it had
opened its doors at 06:30 that morning. The two parents were
in a state of extreme anguish.

Penny, when she arrived, saw them and questioned them
and took statements. Her efforts to calm the Ellis's had had
little effect. A cup of tea had been flung on the floor.
Eventually, with the help of a senior officer in the shape of DI
Carter, they were persuaded to go home, in case their daughter
had returned and then to await developments. Penny promised
them that she would personally make sure that the parents
would be kept in the loop all through the rest of the day.

A counsellor had been sent to their home. It was not an
unfamiliar scene at the busy police station. People get very
angry and upset. It was understandable, of course, Penny had
to try hard not to get emotionally involved. She was the best
of the officers at the station to deal with such cases. She had
been trained to always keep a professional attitude—
otherwise, the stress would be unbearable.

Nevertheless, Penny, who was a caring soul, could not help being upset and Mike and Phippy and other colleagues gathered around her and supported her as best as they could. The case of Kylie Summers was still fresh in everybody's minds at the station. Was this case connected? That was the dread.

At the 10 am briefing, the team was quiet and watching intently. Of course, they all knew there was some bad news coming.

DI Mike Carter strode to the front and cleared his throat. He said, "I know you are all aware of the problem we had early this morning. Another girl was reported missing by her parents, bringing us some awful memories of Kylie Summers' abduction and death a few months ago. At the time we feared that abduction was not the end of the story and it appears our fears may have been well-founded."

Mike poured himself a glass of water and took a drink from it, clearing his throat again. He continued, "What happened last evening was that another young girl appears to have been abducted, although in this case a somewhat older girl of fourteen years, whereas Kylie was just short of thirteen. But the girl who was abducted last night, one Natalie Ellis, was very similar in appearance to Kylie, strong, tall, slim and attractive with long, fair hair.

Natalie was a student at the private girl's school, Rolling-berg High. In this case, the girl's parents are middle-class and have money—her mother owns stables and her father is a financial advisor, but I don't think this abduction, like the last one, has anything to do with money. I very much doubt whether there will be a ransom demand, although it is possible in this case as the parents do have the money to pay such a demand.

Another similarity to Kylie's abduction is that Natalie was out riding her bicycle when she was abducted. She had gone to her school at eight o'clock last night, on her bike and that is the last her parents saw of her, as they waved her off from their house. They had been sent a faked letter offering Natalie some tuition on her oboe—she was a member of the school orchestra.

The letter stated that a member of the Birmingham Symphony Orchestra would be holding a masterclass at her school that evening. It was all false information. We have checked that such a masterclass was not in fact going to take place. Natalie must have been abducted before she got to the school or at least at the school entrance.

The school assured us that it was all locked up securely last night. No one would have been able to access their premises, as far as they were concerned. Of course, the staff and students there are all very upset, too. Penny and I will be visiting the school later today, of course. Right! That's it for now. I will now accept questions."

There was a great shuffling of feet and coughing, but no hand went up. At last, it was DC Ivor "Taffy" Parry who raised his hand.

"Yes, Taff, I know we can rely on you, lad."

"Sir, as this case appears likely to be classed as by a serial perpetrator, will we be helped out again by Rudi, I mean Dr Rudolph Valentine, I know he is over here and staying with DCS Rowles. He was so helpful in the case of 'The Angel of Death', serial murders, a year or so ago, wasn't he? Nobody knows more about the psychological aspects of serial murderers or abductors, see you."

There were murmurs of agreement from the floor. Rudi was so well-liked and respected by all who got to meet him the last time.

DCS Len Rowles was standing at the back of the room. He had entered while Mike was giving his report. He said, in his rumbling, deep voice, "If I can butt in here, Inspector, I'd like to answer this one."

Mike nodded, gratefully.

"My good friend Rudi, as he likes to be called by all, is over here on holiday." He glared at the team and repeated, "On holiday! All right? As many of you know, his wife and baby son were killed in a dreadful accident near his home. We all knew his wife, the wonderful Dr Janet who was our forensic pathologist and we mourn her death greatly. Rudi is here recovering from this terrible tragedy and I am not asking him to help us in our investigations in any way shape or form. I hope that is clear!"

He finished the sentence in a kind of deep roar, looking directly at the pale face of DC Parry, who replied in his lilting Welsh accent, "Yes, Sir, of course. I am sure everyone here would like to express sincere condolences to Rudi. He was and is a well-liked and greatly respected colleague, sir."

There was a round of warm applause from the team. Some stood, some hooted in a very American way. The superintendent looked taken aback, as the applause grew and grew and did not show any sign of stopping. He put his hands in the air and there were tears in his eyes. He too was well loved by his team who would have laid down their lives for the man.

When the applause eventually petered out he spoke, quietly and slowly, "Thank you, Taff. Thank you all—I will pass on your good wishes to Rudi the next time I see him at home."

Mike said, "Penny has completed an excellent report giving the details of the case gathered from interviewing and taking statements from young Natalie's parents, so I will pass the floor over to her. Penny?"

DC Penny Summers stood up and walked to the front, carrying her iPad on which she made her report and notes. Although rather short and on the plump side, Penny had some stunning curves and she had a rather sexy walk. Some of the men crossed their legs and tried not to stare hungrily.

She thanked Mike and then started her report, she had a strong and rather husky voice, deep for a woman.

"Natalie Dawn Ellis, aged just fourteen, described as a tall, well-built, athletic girl with long fair hair. Her school photograph is pinned up behind me and you can see she is a very attractive child. Her parents and her school describe her as a bubbly and very intelligent young lady doing well in her studies, someone who has a bright future ahead of her.

She is well adjusted and socially adept, never in any trouble—a really nice youngster, good at many sports, a member of the school orchestra and a born leader. Her membership of the school orchestra is important, as I shall explain further.

Her mother, Jessica, owns and runs stables for rescued horses. She told me about the fake letter that you have already heard about, falsely inviting her to a masterclass with a member of the Birmingham Symphony Orchestra—a very clever idea by her abductor and showing that he or she, had good knowledge of Natalie and her activities. This perpetrator knew where Natalie lived and could obtain genuine school notepaper on which to fake the letter, which she took with her by request in the wording, so we do not have it as evidence.

So, Natalie, all eager and excited as we can well imagine, was waved off by her parents, riding her bike as she always did when she went to school, hail, rain or snow, so to speak. It was the last they saw of her. Whether she reached the school or what happened next, we do not at this time know, but Natalie literally disappeared somewhere between her home and her school, leaving no trace. I will stop now for questions."

There was much shuffling of feet. Eventually, Detective Sergeant Phipps, who was standing alongside Mike Carter and Len Rowles, spoke up, in his broad black country accent:

"Come on you lot! Put y'owm bloody thinking caps on! It's what we'm paid for!" He glared at the team. He could be quite intimidating when he was aroused. "Orlroyt, orlroyt, I'll start yow off and ask the obvious—Pen—the question is, do you think this case is linked to the abduction and death of young Kylie Thomas or not? I think I know the answer, but we gorra make it clear, mate. Oh and bye the bye, thanks for a grite report, kidder, well done!"

Penny smiled, looking gorgeous, "Sadly, Phippy, I am sure and I know the inspector and the super agree too, that this is the same perpetrator who has taken Natalie as a replacement for Kylie when she became ill and died on him. He needed to find another young girl for whatever twisted purpose we can only guess at. It does not look as if it is a sexual purpose, for which we can be thankful, at least."

DCS Len Rowles glowered at the team. He stood in an aggressive posture and pointed his massive finger at the team. His voice was loud.

"OK. We know the fact of this case thus far. We have another local family with their lives shattered by this monster prowling our streets. You know what you have to do. Find this bastard and bring him to book. Find Natalie and reunite her with her loving family. The Chief Constable is on my back. The public is baying for blood—our blood. **I want action. I want swift action**. All leave is cancelled. I want you to work day and night, tirelessly on this case and I will be watching you all closely!"

He finished on a thundering note, but then became quiet. "Look, I know you are a great team, really good team and together we can do this. Just don't let me down. Don't—let-me-down."

Almost a whisper at the end. The silence was awesome.

After a long glare, he stalked out of the room. DI Mike Carter took his place.

He said, quietly, "There is no doubt that Natalie was abducted at the school. Unfortunately, we have no CCTV images of the school entrance, nor are there any cameras in the immediate vicinity of the school. This is an exclusive private school and there has never been any trouble there so I imagine it has never seemed to be necessary to install security cameras there.

As in the previous case, this perp is thorough and exacting. We have made little if any progression in finding him or her since the Kylie abduction, as you all are aware. It has been very frustrating indeed for all of us, but we are where we are. At least, in this new case, we can at least make some assumption about the monster in our midst, as Penny has already pointed out in her excellent report."

There was another round of warm applause and Penny coloured with pleasure.

At this point, the door of the room opened to reveal a face from the past, Dr Rudolph Valentine! After a moment's stunned silence the room again broke out in applause and hoots of welcome. The team was delighted—and so was Rudi, who strode to the front, stopping to shake hands with those he passed, smiling his famous 1000-watt smile.

However, the familiar remembered glow of health and vitality was much dimmed and there were signs written large on his face of the grief and sorrow he had suffered, without much spoiling his incredible good looks. He stood next to Penny and she gazed up at him with open-mouthed adoration.

All the ladies fancied Rudi like mad! He made the old notion of one's lover being tall, dark and handsome really true, with his dark, glittering eyes and Latin olive skin and his thick, black, wavy hair. His every movement was made with effortless grace. And, amazingly, he was so nice with it, so modest, warm and friendly. A truly outstanding specimen of male beauty—and he's clever—and rich!

Rudi held up his hand, "Hi you guys. That was a great welcome. I really appreciate it, thanks a million. Actually, I just passed your boss on his way out of the meeting and I guess he was as surprised as y'all are to see me here. Well, I'll tell you, I want to help, to get involved. I've missed you guys.

Hey! I had a great time with you, I really did. So I'm back. I'll see if Len will let me have my desk back in his office and I'll be staying on and will be around to chat with you all and catch up with all the news in the next few days. So, thanks again for a great welcome and—hey guys! Let's catch this bastard, OK?"

"Three cheers for Rudi!" rang out, followed by "For he's a jolly good fellow!"

DCS Len had come back in the room and had a grin as wide as a bus. He just stood there nodding his huge bald head benevolently. It was a scene that would be remembered by all who were there that day for the rest of their lives.

Chapter Five

Natalie slowly regained consciousness. She felt awful. She thought she must be in hospital. She knew she was in bed, in a strange room, but she could not focus properly—the room kept swimming and refused to keep still. Her mouth was dreadful, all thick and slimy, but she did not feel frightened, just confused and bewildered. She went back to sleep but was tossing and turning in her bed.

Natalie was under the influence of Flunitrazepam, the drug also called Rohypnol, commonly used to weaken a girl's resistance to sex on a date. It has the effect of relaxing the youngster's body and making her receptive to suggestions. A mind-altering drug, tasteless and usually mixed with alcohol. Simon had injected the drug into the girl earlier, while she was unconscious from the effect of the ether.

Simon had not entered the girl's bedroom since he had undressed her and put her to bed in a luxurious negligee. The bed had silk sheets and pillows. The room was one of the 'pleasure rooms' in his faux 'Roman Baths' leisure centre building, furnished with the utmost sheer luxury money could buy. He had been watching her almost continuously on his CCTV in his lounge at home. He saw that she was awake and so he ran over and entered her room.

He had decided not to allow her to regain consciousness just yet. He wanted to talk to her and start on his plan to win her over, but he could not risk her becoming agitated and hysterical. He wasn't ready to cope with that. He had brought another needle full of Rohypnol with him and he injected the drug into the girl swiftly. She stirred but didn't wake up. He had other mind-altering drugs ready to hand should he need them.

She should sleep for several more hours now, he thought, though he had no real experience to call upon. He was enjoying himself immensely. He had taken a year's sabbatical leave from all his occupations in order to concentrate his efforts solely on his grand plan. His first experiment would be under the heading of Persuasion! No more drugs after this! He needed to talk to her as a next step.

His next step had been carefully planned. He went back to his house to write a letter to Natalie's parents. He did not want them to worry and especially he did not want Natalie to worry about her sister and her parents, so he had to sort out this problem from the start. The letter was simple, printed out from his computer on the Word program:

Dear Mr and Mrs Ellis

I have your daughter. She is well and safe. She will be well looked after and will have all that she needs. She will not be harmed or touched by me, let me assure you. I want her to have a wonderful life with me at her side. I am super rich. She will have every luxury life can offer. Rejoice for her. She is the chosen one!

I want to thank you for bringing this wonderful girl into the world and for raising her so well. But I know you will need to be compensated for her loss. **So, I will pay you the sum of** one million pounds, subject to some conditions which I will inform you about in due course. This offer is not negotiable.

Searching for your daughter will be futile. You may show this letter to the police, but I'm afraid they will not be able to help you.

Yours, with many thanks,

Leo, her new father.

Simon deleted the letter from his computer. He intended to destroy the computer and the printer as soon as he could, as he knew forensics was possible.

Simon put the letter in a stamped and addressed plain brown A5 envelope. He had written the address with his left hand, in capitals. He went out and posted it in Wolverhampton City Centre Main Post Office. Of course, he had worn gloves throughout. He even put on a cap, in case a stray hair fell in or onto the letter. He smiled as he put the letter in the massive post-box built into the wall. He knew he was safe—he was much too clever for the local plods.

Chapter Six

The letter arrived at the Ellis's home the next day. Natalie's big sister took it in, with a couple of other letters, to her mum while she was having her breakfast of porridge and prunes. Ugh! She thought.

Melissa was staying with her mum because of her sister's abduction, being granted the time off from university. They did not speak much about the subject of Natalie's abduction—it was just too difficult—but they gave comfort to each other by just being there together. They tried to act as normal as possible, as it was the only way to cope. Jessica's husband, David, had gone back to work as it was his way of dealing with it, he would have gone mad mooning about the house. He was a good boss and his staff were very fond of him and very pleased he was there back in control.

Jessica sorted through the mail, absently. There were the usual couple of junk letters, from animal food companies, etc. The letter from Simon looked unusual, the first-class stamp and the shaky capital letters. Immediately she suspected it was from the person or persons who had her daughter. She tore it open feverishly and scanned the contents. She gave a little scream and went white and almost fell into a faint. Melissa noticed what was happening and asked her mum what was wrong. Dumbly her mum passed her the letter.

Melissa sat down and read the letter through. She also gave a little scream. She gasped, "It's not true, Mum, it's another fake. Someone is playing a nasty joke on us. I'll tear it up. It's horrible, horrible!"

"No, don't tear it up!" Jessica grabbed it back. "No! we must ring the police—NOW!"

She grabbed the phone and rang the stored police station number in a frenzy. The call went straight through to Mike Carter. He listened intently as Jessica read the contents of the letter to him, in a shaky voice.

The detective inspector said, as calmly as he could manage, though he himself was shaking with excitement. "I'll come round right away, Mrs Ellis. Calm down, this sounds like a good development if it's genuine. Don't handle the letter anymore or the envelope, there may be clues for our science team to find. I'm on my way over right now. This may be a vital breakthrough. I'll be ten minutes. Put the kettle on!"

He grabbed his jacket and sprinted out of the office, just stopping to tell Penny to alert the CSI team. In his jacket pocket, he always carried a selection of evidence bags and a pair of protective gloves.

As soon as he arrived, he donned the gloves and put both the envelope and the letter into two transparent evidence bags and then sat down with the mother and daughter for a chat. He thankfully accepted a cup of tea but refused a biscuit.

He smiled reassuringly at the two women and carefully read the letter through twice, very slowly. He leaned back in the chair and said, "Wow! I've never seen anything like this before! It's amazing!"

Melissa said, "But isn't it just a scam, a sick joke? You don't think it's genuine, surely? Just some nasty, twisted swine indulging himself at our expense!"

Mike said, "I understand where you are coming from, young lady, I really do—but I have a gut feeling that this is genuine, right enough. It fits the pattern of the kind of perpetrator we believe to be responsible for your sister's abduction. This is the first time I have heard of a kidnapper offering compensation, I mean that offer of a million pounds is really extraordinary. But, no, I don't think this is a scam. I think it is genuine, as I say, it fits the pattern, Melissa, isn't it?"

The girl nodded but looked unconvinced. Her mum said, shakily, "So you think, Inspector, that at least my child is alive and unharmed—is that what you think?"

She looked pleadingly at the young man sitting calmly opposite her. Despite herself, she was thinking how handsome he was and how, nice, what a lovely man! She also despised herself for thinking about the million pounds—

Mike said, "I think your daughter will be well looked after by this man. I also think he must obviously be as rich as he says he is by the fact that he is going to give you a million pounds for your daughter. This is not really an offer, it is a statement of intent, but I imagine there will be conditions to be met before he pays up, such as a legal document signed by you and your husband confirming that he is the legal guardian or whatever for Natalie. That will probably follow on soon. Totally illegal of course. Crazy. You can't sell a child!"

He grinned, "Why he wants to do this is the most puzzling aspect to be sorted. Does he want a replacement daughter? Has he lost a beloved daughter? She's only a child, after all.

But he states that his terms and his terms only are on the table, no negotiation on offer. Let's hope the science team can learn something positive from examining this evidence."

He had a calm and smiling face as he sat there.

Melissa burst out, rising to her feet. "It's obscene! Obscene! How can you calmly sit there with a smile on your face and analyse this horrible letter? Fuck the money! Fuck you! I just want my sister back! Do you hear?" She exploded into tears and ran out of the room.

Mike went white with shock. He mentally cursed himself. He had been a fool. A fool! How could he have said all that to the family? Totally unprofessional. He should resign. He felt sick. He staggered to his feet.

"I'm so sorry," he mumbled. "I'll get back to the station."

"No, no, finish your tea. Don't mind Melissa. I must apologise for her behaviour. She is finding it difficult to cope. She's very young. Please don't be upset. You were only trying to help us, dear."

Jessica suddenly felt strong and in charge and she felt really sorry for the young inspector, all her motherly instincts taking over. She felt like giving him a hug and making him better.

Chapter Seven

That early afternoon, DI Mike Carter went to see his boss, DCS Len Rowles who was sitting with Dr Rudi Valentine, in his comfortable office. Mike had printed off some copies of the letter sent to the Ellis family and all three men started off the conference by reading these in silence. Mike had read the letter at least a dozen times, but he dutifully read it again. He was the first to speak.

He said, "One thing I noticed was the grammar that this perp has used. He has an unusual way of expressing the common phrase, 'safe and well' using instead 'well and safe' do you think this is of interest, Rudi, Len?"

Rudi grinned, "Brilliant, Mike—say, you been watching the fascinating serial on English TV about our infamous 'Unabomber' by any chance? I know it has been shown over this side of the pond and it is a great story."

Len looked puzzled for a moment, then his brow cleared, "Oh yes, of course, you mean that guy in America who sent bombs through the post to people he thought were damaging the ecology—your FBI proved he was responsible for the crimes by an analysis of his writing style, is that what you are referring to, Rudi? I saw the programme and, as you say, it was fascinating—but how you found the resources to fund all those agents was equally amazing to me!"

"Yep, got it in one, Len. A most famous case, with a unique method of detection. It's true the FBI had a huge workforce at work on that case, but the pressure to catch that guy was immense, with the President involved. That guy had to be stopped, it was ruining our reputation and it was the postal service for the nation at stake.

But great work, Mike, it's exactly the sort of tool we might have to depend upon if we are to catch this guy, the main purpose of a profile is to inform the questions we ask at interview. If we ask the right questions, we have a much better chance of success."

Mike said, colouring, "Thanks, Rudi. It is true I watched the 'Unabomber' serial or most of it and found it quite amazing, totally fantastic. But I have to make a confession to you both. When I went to see the Ellis family I rabbited on about the case and said a lot of stuff that I really should not have done. I think I was simply showing off—and I'm ashamed of my behaviour. I really am. I'm sorry. It was totally unprofessional of me."

Len looked sympathetic, rather than accusing, he said, "Mm, so what did you say to the family, Mike?"

"I think I said something like the abductor must be a very rich man and that he would not harm Natalie, that he seems to want to buy the girl to maybe replace a daughter who has died and that he will probably want the parents to sign some sort of document agreeing to let him have Natalie before he will pay the million pounds he promises.

I said it was good news as it means the girl is safe and being well looked after. Something on those lines. I really

95

don't know what came over me. The sister flew at me and I don't blame her. I am ashamed of myself. I don't think I should be doing this job." His face had gone grey.

Rudi chimed in, "No, don't be hard on yourself, Mike, I think you were just trying to help the family cope with the trauma and no one can blame you for that. Actually, what you have just said is a great interpretation of the letter and the perpetrator's intentions—absolutely on the ball. We'll make a profiler of you yet. Good work, detective, really good!"

Len said, "I agree, but maybe you should have shown more discretion in discussing the case with the family at this early stage, but I don't think much damage has been done." He paused, then continued, "No, let me rethink this. Sometimes I think we are too damn secretive with families who are grieving, you are a caring and sensitive human being, Mike—and I, for one, like you for that. Sometimes we can take 'professionalism' too far. Don't worry, Mike, you did fine."

Mike whispered, "Thanks, that means a lot to me." His eyes glistened.

Rudi smiled, "Well said, Len, great stuff!" He added, "I think I will attempt a profile on this perpetrator, the letter tells us much more than the contents on display. I will do a full psychological analysis of the letter—I'll get on with it right away—and, truth to tell, I'll thoroughly enjoy myself! As we say on our side of the pond, 'I'm on it'!"

Len laughed and Rudi joined in. Len was delighted to hear Rudi laughing again. He said, "Well, we need to come up with a plan of action for the team, ready for the next meeting, in the morning. Any ideas, Holmes?"

Rudi said, "Well, one thing that is obvious is that we need to do a lot of foot slogging research into the local super rich guys—we need to find out if any such guys has suffered a bereavement, particularly of a daughter. Both of the girls abducted were similar in stature and colouring, similar in being athletic and very attractive. I reckon we should widen the search out to include partners, even friends who may have been really close to the suspect."

Mike said, with a grin, "I'm on it!" to general laughter, especially for Rudi who aimed a playful punch at young Mike. Len thought it was the first time he had seen his friend so relaxed and playful for a long, long time.

Rudi added, "Another thing, you guys, I'm not sure what the situation is over here, but in the States, it would be very difficult to pay someone a big sum of money without revealing identity. If and when this perp pays up we might have a good chance of locating him by tracing the money trail, I reckon."

Len said, "Well that's another task we can give someone at the meeting tomorrow morning. Taffy's a clever lad and this will be right up his street. Good thinking Rudi, we are making progress." He paused, then, "The Game's Afoot, Watson!" he roared, putting on his best upper-class voice.

To more laughter, the three men rose to their feet, signalling the end of the meeting. Anyone less like the conventional image of Sherlock Holmes could not be imagined in the form of the huge and monstrous superintendent!

Chapter Eight

Natalie again stirred. She felt a lot better than last time. More focussed and less ill. The drugs had worn off. She realised, in a confused way, that she was in a bed, in a silver silk negligee and covered with white silk sheets. She rubbed her eyes, trying desperately to make some sense of what was happening to her.

She saw that she was surrounded by utter luxury, that she was in a sort of fairy-tale bedroom massive in size and furnished with the most sumptuous and elegant furniture, with a colour scheme of soft pinks and greys. Several tall windows were hung with velvet curtains and delicate white gauze was blowing gently in a cool breeze that was scented with wood pine. On the floor was thick white fluffy carpet. Background music was playing—an *oboe concerto by Debussy*.

As her eyes cleared, she was amazed to see, on a sort of chaise-longue, an elegant young man reclining and smiling at her. It was Simon, of course. He had been observing her on CCTV and had noticed she was stirring. He knew the drugs that he had injected were by now wearing off. He wanted to speak to her and tell her of his plans for her future.

He was dressed in a yellow silk jacket, black tee-shirt and blue trousers. His shoes were white and he wore a white silk scarf loosely knotted around his neck. He thought he looked just perfect for the impression he had created of a fantasy world of pleasure and beauty. A handsome prince. He was ecstatic with excitement and totally at ease with his master plan. It could not fail—surely a young girl would be swept off her feet and be like putty to be shaped to his desires.

He was tempted to go and kiss the girl—carrying on with his romantic fantasy of the sleeping beauty being awoken by the handsome prince. He got off his sofa and went over to her and bent over her, puckering up his lips. She looked at him with horror and beat her fists on his face.

"What are you doing, you pervert!" she shrieked. "I know you. You're Dr Shaw, the conductor. Where am I?" Her eyes opened wide, "YOU BEAST! You've kidnapped me. HELP! HELP!" she started to scream and struggled to get out of the bed. She pushed him hard and ran to the door. It would not open.

Simon was aghast! This was not at all what he expected! He did not know what to do. He grabbed the struggling girl and threw her back onto the bed. Grabbed a pillow and put it over her mouth and nose. Natalie kicked her legs strongly and Simon had to kneel on the girl's chest to hold her down.

He was sobbing and screaming, "BE QUIET—OH PLEASE! WHY WON'T YOU BE QUIET! OH PLEASE! YOU BEAUTIFUL GIRL. PLEASE! DON'T YOU WANT TO BE A PRINCESS? I LOVE YOU I LOVE YOU I LOVE YOU! STOP STRUGGLING! PLEEEASE! OH, GOD! BE **QUIET!**"

After a while, she went quiet.

Chapter Nine

At 9 o'clock the next day, Rudi, Len and Mike were in conference, planning for that morning's 10 am briefing.

Rudi said, "Hey, you guys got any results from the research into rich people who may have been in contact with young Natalie?"

Mike grinned, "Well it certainly isn't going to be one of the teaching staff at Rollingberg High, Rudi—they earn even less than us coppers on the whole. I can't see any one of them being able to afford to offer one million quid for the purchase of a pretty girl and I can't believe I just said that!"

Len commented, "Rollingberg High is a great school with a great reputation in the area, private of course and exclusive. We have never heard of any problems there no matter how far we look in our records. I think we can discount there being a millionaire on the staff, but we must also consider that the offer in the letter was not truthful so we must treat all the staff there as possible suspects, after all the perpetrator knew a lot about the school and how it operates, the paper the letter was printed on was a genuine school item.

He or she knew Natalie well enough to know she played the oboe in the school orchestra and knew her address and that she cycled to school. That is a lot of knowledge to have for an outsider."

Rudi said, "Yes, Len, that's obvious and we must consider it, but I really think this is a genuine letter, from a genuine rich guy, it feels that way to me. A gut feeling maybe, but a very strong one. Apart from the staff, there must be local businessmen and others, including parents, with good knowledge of what goes on.

Back in the USA most of the funding for schools comes from rich business tycoons and families. I myself have a relationship with a local high school and have made regular donations for various purposes over the years."

Mike said, "You're the expert, Rudi, I have every faith in you, mate. You must guide us through this, 'cause frankly, I haven't a clue."

Rudi laughed, "You know the definition of an expert— from 'ex'—a has-been and 'spurt' a drip under pressure!"

The three men all laughed out loud. Len looked affectionately at his American friend and thought how lovely it was to hear him tell a joke.

Rudi added, "No, to be serious, my friends, I really *feel* this guy, who I think is suffering from what is probably a severe psycho-symptomatic condition leading to paranoid delusions of a fantasy world of his or her own making. This makes him or her extremely dangerous and someone we must catch before he or she kills again and again in search of the unattainable."

"Wow! You've lost me there!" said Mike, admiringly.

Len added, "Unattainable, Rudi?"

"Yes, Len, unattainable in that I think what this perpetrator is looking for is a replacement female for one that he has lost and that is *impossible*—it just cannot be done."

"Crikey Moses!"

Len thought for a minute or two then said, "Are we thinking of brainwashing here, Rudi, I mean is this perpetrator going to try to change Natalie's way of thinking, so that she accepts him—and I think we are talking about a male here—as a lover or father or whatever?"

"Certainly not brainwashing, Len. But you're right—the perpetrator is almost certainly a male, reinforced by the fact that he is abducting females, of course. So from now on, I'll just use a masculine word to describe him. No, brainwashing was a concept for changing the way a person thinks, using torture and suchlike, there's no way he can achieve what he wants by such a method.

I don't think our guy is that stupid—no, he will use his wealth and influence to try to persuade a girl to come over to him willingly—at least that has some chance of success, but I cannot see him ever attaining his goal, really. It's not on, Len, just not on."

Mike said, "It all the depends on the girl herself. I can see some girls being persuaded perhaps by the chance to be another Kim Kardashian living in a fantasy world of glamour and celebrity—you've only got to look at the rows of magazines for women on the supermarket shelves to see how popular such lives are."

"True. You're right on there, Mike. I'm amazed at what I see on those shelves, but these are dreams and not reality for the ladies who love to read about these so-called celebrities and all their problems. There's no way they want that sort of lifestyle for themselves, I don't imagine. Not really. No.

He will fail—and then he will have to kill Natalie in order to escape justice. Like many very rich and influential guys, he cannot imagine failure. They are surrounded by toadies who agree with every word he utters. He will then seek another girl. He will never stop until he succeeds."

Len half-rose from his chair. "Yes, indeed, Rudi. Masterly. But Mike! We need to catch this bastard before that happens!"

He crashed his immense fist on the desk, his red nose quivering alarmingly. Mike and Rudi hurriedly left the office. They all headed for the briefing room, as 10 o'clock loomed.

The atmosphere in the room was tense. Len, Mike and Rudi strode to the front. Len opened the meeting and greeted the team warmly. Rudi once more was greeted with a round of applause and flashed his amazing smile that lit up the room. Probably only Mike, who was a film buff, knew of his namesake the huge star of the silent movies back in the 1920s, the great romantic megastar, Rudolph Valentino, but the name was appropriate for Rudi's tall, dark and handsome looks and magnetic aura.

Mike then asked Detective Constable Ivor Parry, known as 'taffy', to come to the front, introducing him as the officer leading the research into possible rich contacts of the victim, Natalie Ellis.

Taffy came out and stood before the team, a smile on his fierce-looking face. Although small in stature he had considerable 'presence' with his aggressive jutting beard, glittering deep-set eyes and thick black eyebrows. A fiery Welshman, tough as they come and a terror in a rugby game.

With his university background and a degree in Law, he was headed for the top and he knew it.

He glanced down at his iPad and said, in his lilting Welsh accent, "Thanks, sir. Yes, my team has done a lot of research on that topic and I think you all be surprised at what we have managed to discover. Of course, all the staff at Natalie's school are automatically suspects, but none of them are rich, nor, as far as we can determine so early in the investigation have any of the staff suffered the loss of a loved one recently—the two main tick boxes that we were looking for, see you."

When Taffy was excited, as he was now, his Welsh syntax became more apparent. He continued, "However, Natalie's school is a private, fee-paying one, so the parents are generally well-off middle-class types and when I looked at the Board of Governors of the school there are quite a few millionaires among them.

Now, see you, I don't know if you know much about the management of schools, I certainly didn't, like, but all schools, Local Authority or private, are governed by a Board of Governors, which in the case of Local Authority schools commonly called Council Schools; they have Councillors on the Board, like, plus the head teacher or principal of the school, plus parents and volunteers who devote their time and talents to help govern the school to the best of their ability, doing their bit for the local community, like."

The young detective paused and looked around the room. He was aware of shuffling feet. Taffy was not a popular member of the team, as most regarded him as an arrogant 'know-all'. He said, uncertainly, "I hope I'm not boring you with all that."

Len butted in, "No, no, lad, you're doing fine. Carry on!" He glared at the assembled team and they inwardly quaked.

"Thank you, sir. I'll go straight to the millionaires then. I've picked out a few of the more obvious candidates from the governors. One in particular that I'll start off with." The room became very quiet as they all eagerly waited.

"Well, see actually Natalie's school, er, Rollingberg High?—have a Finance Sub-Committee which reports back to the main board, see. They meet once a term to examine and control the School finances, including the fees to be paid, salaries, maintenance of the building, etc, etc, you know the sort of thing. Anyway, on that committee sit some really well-off men and women and one of them has also suffered a recent loss of a daughter, much the same age as Natalie!"

Taff looked around triumphantly, as this last piece of information went down like a bombshell with all the team really sitting up and taking notice.

Mike, Len and Rudi joined in the warm applause. Taff grew rather red in the face. However, he continued gamely, "This guy, who is divorced, lives in a huge manor house as far as I can gather and his daughter, Dawn, who lived with him, had been suffering from a brain tumour for some time and treatments didn't work, even though she travelled to America at huge cost. The poor young girl died some nine or ten months ago."

Mrs Bowyer, the civilian minutes secretary, murmured, "Do we have the name of this person, please?"

"Sure. I was coming to that. The guy's name is a Mr Selwyn Plant. He is the owner, chairman and MD of Plant Homes Ltd, a company which builds housing estates all around the Midlands—I'm sure you've all heard of them and seen their advertising boards dotted around. I bet, see, some of you live in a house his company built, see!" There was a murmur of agreement in the room.

As the talking increased, Mike butted in loudly, "So this Selwyn Plant becomes our Prime Suspect, perhaps."

Phippy added, to laughter, "Arr, he's our *only* bloody suspect as well!"

Rudi said, "Well said, Phippy, a good laugh, but this is a most important development, as I'm sure you are all aware—without suspects we are on a voyage to nowhere. And this guy ticks all our boxes—brilliant work, detective!"

The sound of an aircraft low overhead drowned out everything at that point. The station stood directly on the flight path to Birmingham Airport and every fifteen minutes or so in normal times the building seemed to shake as a jet roared overhead, coming into land. Since the Pandemic the number of times this happened had plummeted, however.

Len said, "I think we must go and see this man, Selwyn Plant, today if we can manage it—at least we should try. Fix it, will you Mike." It wasn't a question.

Taff said, uncertainly, "there are several other possibilities, sir. Shall I carry on?"

The super grinned, "Sorry Constable. Yes, carry on son, you're doing great."

So the young Welshman continued, "Thank you, I think I did my best, as you all do all the time, we are a great team." He paused, hoping for more applause, but none was forthcoming so he hurriedly carried on.

"Yes, well, as I said, besides Mr Plant, we have several other governors all on the finance committee unsurprisingly, who are, I think, capable of offering the sort of monetary inducements being offered to Natalie's parents. For example, we have Jimmy Brewer, who we have all seen on the telly ads promoting his mini supermarkets all over the place, undercutting all the big supermarkets and offering all sorts of dubious deals and bargains to his customers.

Big Jimmy, as he likes to be called, is a larger-than-life character, very loud and pushy, a total extravert, see. All this is hearsay, by the way, I have not met any of these people, you understand. I've just read archive local newspapers and magazines, but the school itself was very helpful to me. I don't know if Mr Brewer has suffered any family bereavements, he might have or might not have, I just don't know, like."

Taff paused again and drank some water from a bottle he'd brought in with him. He smiled and carried on gamely, "Then there's Sir Charles Frazer, golf club owner, online golf shops, yacht owner, spends a lot of time in exotic locations, but is very active as a governor of the school and has two daughters studying there.

He acts as an unpaid golf coach at the school, so meets a lot of the students. However, I don't think Sir Charles is much of a possibility, see, but one never knows. He is tough and handsome and has the reputation of being a Ladies' Man."

He noticed a certain amount of coughing and shuffling of feet, so he paused yet again and looked around, grinning.

"All right, all right, look you. There is just one more, lastly like, there is Fred Last, appropriately, wealthy garage proprietor, mainly second-hand, again seen on local television, another larger-than-life character, jolly and fat, but very involved with the school where he arranges trips and holidays, such as skiing trips to Austria and France, so he knows a lot of the girls personally. Well, that's it—thanks for listening. I've cut it short at bit, but if you have any questions, I will try to answer them."

Taff gulped some more water from his bottle of Welsh Spring Water. There were no questions. Mike thanked the young man and there was another handsome round of applause as he returned to his seat among the team. He got a few slaps on the back as walked back, much to his pleasure. He knew he was not normally a popular team member and consoled himself that it was probably envy!

DC Penny Summers then gave a report on Natalie's friends at school and background information about the Ellis family, including both the mother and the father and about Melissa, Natalie's 20-year-old elder sister, currently at university studying for a business studies degree.

Penny than added, "One Governor of the School that Taff didn't mention was a man called Dr Prof. Simon Shaw." She grinned at Taff, who protested, "I ran out of time. Anyway, he did not strike me as being a possible suspect, I mean, doctors are well paid, but hardly multi-millionaires, Pen—plus he was not on the Finance Committee!"

"Ah, true, but wait a minute, Taff, Simon Shaw is chairman of the main board, is the son and heir to the rather famous socialite Maggie Shaw, who was from a fabulously rich background. Her grandfather was an armaments mogul who made a fortune from the first world war, her father made another fortune on the stock market and Maggie, as the only child, inherited the lot when her father died.

You might remember in the papers last year about Maggie when she was killed riding her immensely powerful motorbike at over hundred miles an hour down the M6

Motorway. I think the young doctor should include in your list, matey. He probably has assets and shares worth at least a hundred million pounds—oh and he is a guest conductor and mentor of the school orchestra.

Now, Natalie played in the orchestra, so Dr Shaw must have known her quite well. Remember the letter to Natalie which led to her abduction was a false invitation to a meeting with a member of Birmingham Symphony Orchestra!" Taff mumbled something hard to catch, but he was not pleased. The two young coppers were very much in competition at the station.

Rudi said, "Hey, Pen, that guy sounds really interesting. Perhaps you and I should go see him this afternoon?" Penny nodded her head, turning scarlet with delight and longing—she just could not believe her luck! She stumbled back to her seat amid wild applause. There were several hugs and pats to cope with.

The reports came to an end after some which covered the history of the school, a rundown of the teaching staff and some research into the school orchestra. The team were then allocated jobs and told, by Len, in no uncertain terms to "Get on with it!"

Len and Mike prepared to go and interview Mr Selwyn Plant, after lunch in the local pub. They invited Taff to go with them, as a necessity. He was delighted, of course. He pulled a face at Penny, but she ignored him. Rudi had invited Penny to lunch with him at the same venue—she knew whose company she preferred!

Chapter Ten

Rudi and Penny borrowed a car from the police vehicle stock and made the journey to Simon Shaw's estate.

Penny did the driving. On the journey, Rudi at first was very quiet and Penny just said standard things about the weather and about the district they were driving through. She told him that Simon lived in South Staffordshire, almost on the border with Shropshire in a very rural part of the West Midlands. She knew the area quite well because she had a sister living the large village of Codsall, some six miles from Wolverhampton and again close to the border of Shropshire.

Rudi admired the narrow, winding country roads and the soft hills and multi-coloured small fields, some verdant with golden flowering rape, with hedges bursting out with snowy-white May blossom. He found it very restful for his damaged soul. Although he never for one minute could stop grieving for his wife and baby son, the beauty of Nature brought some much-needed solace.

As they neared the end of their journey Simon spoke, "Penny," he said, "This sure is a beautiful part of the world. I don't think you folk truly appreciate what you have got in this little island—it is a sort of Paradise on Earth."

Penny looked at him, her eyes becoming moist. She said, "I know—it really is breath-taking around here at this time of the year. But, oops, I think we have arrived. Wow!"

It was just around a sweeping bend they had their first view of the magnificent wrought iron gates fronting the Victorian property. The hawthorn hedges were at least three metres high and stretching far into the distance either side of the massive, elaborate gates, painted black and gold.

Penny stopped the car and switched off the engine. They got out and approached the gates. They did not have an appointment as it was deemed important to arrive unexpectedly. It was about 06:45 pm and they hoped Simon might be home. There was a black metal post with a built-in speaker and a button to press, so Penny pressed it.

Nothing happened. Penny pressed it again. And again. All with a similar negative response. She shrugged her shoulders and got out her mobile phone from her handbag. She had programmed Simon's personal number, obtained from the school, into the phone. So she entered the number. It rang and continued ringing for several minutes and then went on to a messaging service, annoyingly. She did not answer.

Rudi said, "I reckon we are on CCTV, Pen. There is a miniature camera hidden among the gate's fancy ironwork. Video and sound monitors, very high-tech, as far as I can judge."

Penny rolled her eyes. "Well, now what do we do?"

"I really don't know, Pen, I guess we need to consider our options." He grinned at the young constable and she felt her knees go weak.

He motioned for her not to speak, then whispered in her ear. "Someone is probably listening to us, as well as watching us, so be careful what you say."

At that moment the speaker in the post crackled to life. It was Simon, who had made an instant decision to get this thing over right away. He had a good idea the two visitors were likely to be police. He said, "Dr Shaw's residence, hello, how can I help you? Sorry to keep you waiting."

Penny got out her ID and showed it. "Oh hello. Police. Just a courtesy call. I am Constable Summers and this is Dr Valentine, who is assisting the local police at this time. We are simply making enquiries about the disappearance of one of the pupils at the school, Natalie Ellis. Dr Shaw is chairman of the Governors of the school as I am sure you are aware."

Simon interjected, "I am Dr Shaw."

"Oh, sorry sir, well, as I was saying, Dr Shaw, we are making enquiries and we would like very much to ask you a few questions. Could we come in and meet you, please? I realise we have to be careful about Covid infections, but if we all wear masks and socially distance ourselves, we should be reasonably safe and following the government guidelines."

"I know all about Covid. I nearly lost my life to it only recently. You may have read about it in the Press. But, yes, I will open the gates and meet you at the front of the house. You will need to drive, as it about a mile away along the drive. I really cannot imagine how I can help you but if you must, you must. Just for a few minutes, though, I am very busy."

There was a loud click and the big gates noiselessly opened.

The drive was long and winding, with high hedges obscuring any view, but eventually, they came out into a wide section of drive in front of the house. As they arrived Simon came bouncing down the many steps to meet them, a warm smile on his boyish, tousled-hair face.

He greeted them charmingly. He thought Rudi was absolutely gorgeous and rather ignored Penny. He stuck out his elbow as the norm handshake substitute and Rudi complied first and then the diminutive Penny, reaching high. Simon spoke first.

"Welcome you guys, how can I help? I know it is a dreadful business. I do know the girl in question vaguely. I think she plays the oboe rather well in the school orchestra. I act as a musical advisor to the orchestra and occasionally conduct, especially when it gives a concert.

One does one's best, of course. I am chair of the school governors, for my sins, following on from my dear departed mother. The school orchestra is rather good for its type, but one has to make allowances. But I really can't imagine how I can help." He appeared to be gabbling somewhat, thought Rudi, maybe a sign of nervousness.

Rudi said, "Sir, It was because of her music that Natalie was abducted, as she came to the school on that evening following a letter which invited her to attend a masterclass with an oboe player from the Birmingham Symphony Orchestra. In fact, this was not the case at all, as I am sure you are aware. You, sir, presumably have access to the school premises, as chair of the governors and you are connected with the orchestra and the players. This makes you a person of interest to the police."

"What?" Simon looked amazed.

Penny said, "We must ask you to accompany us back to the station for an interview, Sir."

"Oh really! This is nonsense. Me, a suspect? I will do no such thing!" He had grown red in the face. Somewhere in the distance, a cuckoo was calling.

"We can insist, sir. But if you prefer, we can interview you here and now. We will need a statement from you and details of your movements on the day in question when the victim was abducted, probably from the school premises."

Penny got out her notebook and looked expectantly at Simon.

"Oh well, I suppose you know what you're doing. You had better come around to the patio at the back of my house. There are some tables and chairs, I can rustle up some coffee if you like. Please follow me."

Simon set off at a brisk pace. It was quite a long trek, but eventually, they wound their way around to the rear of the house, where they found a huge Victorian Conservatory and a terraced patio containing some wicker tables and chairs. At the rear of the terraces, a long lawn stretched far into the distance, down to a group of poplars which hid from view the remainder of the grounds.

Simon indicated where the group should sit and went off to make some coffee. (He mentally was kicking himself for having made the offer, but thought it might give him time to think about the situation. He was seriously worried).

Simon no longer had any live-in staff, as a precaution. He could not trust them to not find out about his prisoner in the leisure centre building. So he had to switch on his coffee maker and put out some crockery on a silver tray. He added a plate of vegan oatmeal biscuits. His mind raced as he worked feverishly at his task.

At least he now had a few minutes to prepare himself. His pulse was racing and he was sweating, which he hated. The cuckoo sounded louder now, which also irritated him. He could have cheerfully throttled the creature.

He picked up the loaded tray and wearing his best, most hospitable smile, went out to face the music, on the terrace. Rudi and Pen looked comfortably relaxed in the pale late afternoon sunshine and were chatting amiably while admiring the view.

They were well impressed by the beauty of the scene and said as much to their host as he placed the tray on the large wicker coffee table at which they sat. They chatted for a few minutes about the scene and the area while Simon did the honours and they all munched on the biscuits and drank their rather good coffee.

"Now," said Simon brightly, "What do you want to know? Ask me anything you like and I will do my best to answer, I promise. And it will be the truth, the whole truth and nothing but the truth, s'welp me guv's."

He put on a silly voice for the last bit and his guests dutifully laughed.

Penny said, "Thank you, sir. Firstly, can you give us a rundown on your movements on the day Natalie was abducted, 23 April this year?"

Simon gave a rueful chuckle, "Easy to answer, Constable. I was here all day engaged in writing a biography of my mother. I have been advised not to leave my home as a vulnerable person, while this pandemic is raging around us. I have literally not left my house since I left hospital in early March. Frankly, I am bored out of my skull!"

Rudi and Penny looked at each other. Rudi said, "I am sure sorry to hear that, sir, I can understand how you must feel, like a prisoner in your own house."

"Absolutely." Simon rolled his eyes, looking suitably sad. He was a frustrated thespian who considered he was a big loss to the acting profession. Since his schooldays at Eton (of course), where he always played a leading role in any theatrical productions, he had been unable to pursue an acting hobby, as an amateur, as he would not consider a bit part, only a lead, which hardly won him any friends in the amdram world.

Penny said, "For the record, sir, can you prove that you did not leave your home on the day in question? Is there no one who could confirm this?"

"Ah, I see. You mean—have I an alibi for the day?"

"We need to be thorough, sir, A child's life is at stake, perhaps. Are you not concerned, sir?"

Simon laughed out loud, which rather irritated Penny. She thought he was patronising her and that always made her furious.

"Alright, alright. Mea culpa. I am sorry if I seem unconcerted about the girl but really the idea of me having anything to do with this abduction is ludicrous. You know, your Chief Constable was a regular visitor here when my mother was alive and I know him personally. I'm sure he'll vouch for me if asked.

No, to answer your question I am afraid there is no one I can recollect calling on me that day or indeed hardly any other day. I have very few visitors these days. Of course, I have deliveries, such as from Waitrose for groceries. A firm of gardeners comes regularly. But no, I can't see how I can prove that I did not go out on the day in question, I do not even keep a diary to look up the date. I will check my phone for you, hang on a bit."

He got out his phone and pressed a few keys. He looked very sad. "No, no, nothing at all on that date, I'm sorry to say."

Rudi said, "To tell you the truth, Dr Shaw, we have made almost no progress in our investigation thus far and we are frankly clutching at straws, but would it be possible for us to have a quick tour of your house and grounds here, just to be, as my colleague here has said, as thorough as possible, given the circumstances?"

Simon went silent. His face changed. Rudi thought to himself that the man looked frightened. He said, "Oh no, I cannot allow that. You may be carrying the virus with you even if you are asymptomatic. No, I am sorry but the answer to that question is no."

He looked at the two investigators with something like a pleading expression on his young face.

Penny said, "We can obtain a court order if necessary, sir."

"I rather doubt that, but if that is what you must do, then that is what you must do. I must ask you to leave now. I am very busy and I have been more than cooperative, you must agree." He got up and led Penny and Rudi back to their car.

In the car, Penny said, "Of course, Rudi, he is quite right. We have absolutely no chance of convincing a judge that we need to search his house and grounds, with no evidence whatsoever. The super would not hear of it, either. This guy is rich and powerful and no doubt has powerful friends in high places."

Rudi said, "I reckon." He grinned at the downcast constable. "Hey, I think we made good progress here, this guy needs to be investigated thoroughly. He's hiding something and I can sense he has some mental health issues. We need to find out all about Dr Shaw, what makes him tick. Interview people who know him—his friends, his colleagues, his minions, the other governors of the school, the lot, Pen. I have a feeling it will be very revealing. Hey, let's find a café. I fancy a nice cup of tea!"

Penny's knees trembled violently.

Chapter Eleven

The Ellis stables, owner Jessica Ellis, were very quiet on a Monday morning, a few weeks later. The weekend had been, as usual, busy with children and mothers, even the odd father, enjoying the horses. Grooming them, cuddling them, helping to feed them and learning to ride them.

There were three horses, all nice, quiet, obedient mares, a black and white one called Jenny, a brown one called Princess and a white one called Snowball. All much loved and well cared for. But they were out being exercised, as they were every early morning, being ridden that morning by Jessica herself and two of her volunteer staff, so the stables were empty.

A small, but heavy-set young man was left in charge. His name was John and he was a Down's syndrome man, aged thirty-five. He was capable of answering the telephone and was usually a very happy and useful member of staff, strong and able to do a lot of useful tasks around the stable. That morning he had cleaned out all the stalls and put down fresh straw.

He smiled happily as the horses returned, their flanks steaming and he greeted Jessica with a hoarse and deep, slow, monotone voice. "Did you have a nice ride, Mrs Ellis?"—his usual greeting. He could ride the horses himself and was very proud of that.

"It was lovely, John, thank you."

John continued, "There was a delivery for you." He nodded, gravely.

"Oh, I wasn't expecting a delivery today. What is it, John?"

"They're in the office. They were heavy."

"Oh right. Thanks, John. I'll go and have a look in a minute when I've seen to Snowball. Will you settle him down, love—and give him a feed while I go?"

"All right."

Jessica thanked the young volunteer and walked into her office. There were six silvery-grey sacks each tied very tightly with strong cord. She looked puzzled, but lifted one of them and heaved it up onto her desk. There was no address label on any of the sacks. She took a Stanley knife from her desk tidy pot and hacked determinedly at the cord, eventually managing to open one of the sacks.

There was another sack inside it so she opened that too. She peered inside. There were lots of what looked like plastic boxes each about 6cm square. She took one of them out and laid it on the desk. It contained a gold coin. She looked at the coin and saw that it was produced by the Royal Mint.

There was an engraving of Britannia on one side. The lettering on the plastic box stated "One Troy Ounce." Her mind in a whirl she counted the coins in the one sack. There were 105, all exactly the same.

She picked up the phone and dialled her husband.

David was very excited at the news. "My holy aunt! Those are gold Britannias, Jes. You say there are six sacks, so that's, what, 630 Britannias. Darling, they are worth around £1,500 each at least. He's paid up. The abductor. There's a million quid there on your desk! Wow! Stay there, don't move. I'm on my way over!"

"Shall I ring the police?"

"No. We need to think this through! Sit tight!"

Jessica thought, "Please God—surely this must mean Natalie is still alive!"

She went to find John. She asked, "Who delivered those sacks, John love?"

"A man." He looked annoyed. He did not like being questioned. He got confused.

"What sort of a man?"

"I don't *know*," John said, firmly and slowly. He went to walk away.

"Hang on, John. This man did you know him?"

"No. I didn't. He was just a man. He came in a van." He said this loudly and impatiently.

"John, this is important! Try and remember. Tell me what happened."

"It was a man. I helped him carry the sacks. They were heavy." John began to look flustered and upset.

He shouted. "It was just a man! I don't know anymore!" He walked away, his face twisted and angry.

Chapter Twelve

At the Ellis's home, there was a letter waiting for them. It had come by the normal daily post. The address was in shaky capitals again. The letter read:

Your daughter is dead. I am sorry, but she attacked me and I lost my temper defending myself. This was the last thing I wanted. All my plans for her have been ruined. She was my chosen one. If she had listened to me her life would have been one of fabulous joy. But it was not to be.

I chose the wrong girl again, but I will succeed next time, never fear. I have learned from this and I now know what to do. You will have received gold bullion to the value of one million pounds in compensation for the loss of your daughter, as promised. All this money is legally yours. It was simply a business transaction. I wish you well in the future. Leo.

Jessica clutched her husband and wailed with grief. "I don't believe him! He has our daughter locked away somewhere. We must tell the police, David, we must tell the police. Natalie is not dead. She is not! She's not!"

David's face was set. He had no intention of telling the police about the gold. He patted his wife's back and made shushing noises to comfort her. Of course, he was devastated that his precious daughter was dead. He thought the letter told the truth.

He could understand his wife refusing to believe her little girl was dead, of course he did, but he was a financial advisor by profession and a qualified accountant by training and money was his passion. The gold was entering his soul and consuming it with desire. He loved it. He reasoned it was no use trying to bring his daughter back from the dead. He would have to cope with it.

He foresaw a lot of trouble from his wife and a huge amount of trouble from his daughter over this gold. But he would not give it up without a struggle!

He had brought the six sacks home and he longed to empty them all out and run all those gold Britannias through his fingers, but that would not do while his wife was there with him. He would need to think. Be careful. Plan ahead.

He made them both a cup of tea. He took it to her where she lay on a sofa, then he hid the sacks of gold at the top of his wardrobe. Best out of sight and out of mind, of his wife, he thought.

He found it was difficult to think about Natalie. The gold was consuming all his thoughts.

He went and knelt down beside her and held her hand, thinking furiously all the while, wondering what to do, what to say. Don't rush it, he told himself. Play it by ear. Talk of anything except the gold. Or just stay quiet and see what she says first. She had her eyes closed and was pale and drawn.

She said, "I have upset John."

"What do you mean?"

"John, down at the stables. I upset him, questioning him about who delivered those sacks. He hates being questioned."

"Oh, the 'Downs Syndrome' guy. Was it him that saw the sacks delivered, then?"

"I was out exercising the horses, with Jill and Judy, our volunteers. John was holding the fort all by himself this morning. Staff was the four 'j's' as usual."

"So what did John say?"

"He said a man in a van delivered the sacks, but he did not know any more than that. I think he felt he had let me down by not knowing anymore. That's why he was upset."

David saw an opportunity. He said, eagerly, "Then I don't think it would be fair on the lad bringing in the police at the moment. They will want to question John closely about the delivery and imagine how upset that will make him, Jes!"

"I know. That's what I was thinking, too. But won't we get into trouble with the police for, I don't know, withholding evidence or something?"

"Of course not! Don't worry about that. I am sure they don't need to know anything about this at this time. We have to think it all out carefully. What we do, dear. Leave it to me, I will make some enquiries."

He patted her hand. She was the type of woman that depended completely on her husband and was used to 'going along' with everything he wanted to do. "If he's happy, I'm happy" was her mantra.

"Don't leave me, David. I need you here."

"He had no intention of leaving that fantastic hoard of gold in his wardrobe. He knew exactly what to do with it. It was his job. With this hoard, he was made for life! He would, in time, turn that million into ten million!"

Chapter Thirteen

DC Ivor (Taff) Parry, DI Mike Carter and his boss, DCS Len Rowles, arrived at the mansion house of Mr Selwyn Plant, owner, MD and Chairman of Plant Homes just after 3 pm After a pleasant lunch where Taff said very little as he was in awe to some extent to be at the same table as the Chief Super, but the two senior ranks made sure they included the young man in their conversation.

Taff was given the job of driver on this occasion, he would not be interviewing the suspect, rather he would wait in the car. The vast and rather ugly house was in a very secluded and up-market area and little could be heard apart from the noise of a lawn mower somewhere not too far away, no doubt being operated by a paid gardener.

The owners of such properties didn't often have much to do in their gardens, apart from sitting in them occasionally. Even the birds observed silent respect it appeared, as none could be heard chirping. The two senior men had decided to arrange an appointment with Mr Plant, on this occasion and they had arrived a little early, as the appointment was not until 03:15.

Mike couldn't see a bell push, so he raised the big brass knocker on the massive front door and gave it a tentative knock. It was answered almost immediately by a large, untidy-looking man with flowing locks of white hair—none other than Selwyn Plant himself, recognisable from the adverts for his homes.

He said, "Hello, can I help you?" in a soft and courteous voice. Len and Mike were rather surprised and looked at each other.

Mike said, "Right. Well, sir, this is Detective Chief Superintendent Rowles and I am Detective Inspector Carter, from City Police. We have an appointment at 03:15, sir, with you."

Mr Plant inclined his leonine head slightly and motioned for the two men to come through. He said, "Yes, so I believe. With reference to Rollingberg Girls' High School and the missing pupil, Natalie Ellis?"

Len rumbled, "Exactly so, Mr Plant. It is very good of you to agree to see us at such short notice."

"No doubt you have your reasons, gentlemen. Please follow me in my study. I have ordered some coffee for 03:30."

Mike, for something to say, said, "Rather cold for the time of the year, isn't it, sir? Coffee would be very welcome."

Len rumbled something unintelligible.

Mr Plant said nothing. He walked quickly on.

The interior of the house was very plain and rather disappointing. It was rather cold and uninviting. Selwyn's study was the first door on the left of the vast hall. The room was plain, square and very masculine. There was a very large uncluttered wooden desk with a similarly-large leather chair behind and someone had placed two uncomfortable-looking wooden chairs facing the rear of the desk.

The plate-glass window was partly covered by large, dusty-looking pale green curtains, so the light was not good. Mr Plant went and sat at his desk and indicated for the two policemen to sit opposite him. He smiled expectantly at them as they settled themselves as best they could.

"So—how can I help?"

Len said, "Inspector Carter?" Dropping him in it, so to speak, thought Mike.

"Just a courtesy call, sir, as you are one of the school governors. To be frank, sir, we are making almost no headway into our investigations into the disappearance of Natalie Ellis and we are engaged in interviewing anyone from the School that may know the girl at all and, I must tell you that you are ticking some of the boxes in the profile we have of a potential abductor."

"Oh really, how so, exactly."

Len came to the rescue. "We have made use of the services of an expert FBI profiler who has come to help us in our quest. The profile suggests that the abductor is a very wealthy man who has suffered a grievous loss of a female member of his family. We believe that you have recently lost a daughter in very tragic circumstances and may I say, that we are aware that this must be a traumatic and horrible experience for any parent to suffer."

"Ah, I see. So I am a suspect. Is this the case?"

"Rather a person of interest, Mr Plant."

"Ah, yes. A person of interest then. So what can I tell you?"

Mike had to admire the coolness of this guy!

Unexpectedly, Selwyn grinned.

He said, "You know, I must tell you I am delighted to have you two senior detectives as company. You might not realise it, but I am very interested in criminal psychology and I read detective novels by the ton. To find myself a 'person of interest' as you put it, is really a dream come true and has quite made my day!"

Len said, "That makes out job a lot easier, sir. But, for a start, could you tell us something about your daughter?"

"Very well. It is a subject close to my heart. At this time, I am in the process of setting up a charity in her name, to raise funds for research into childhood brain tumours. That was the problem we had to face, detectives, years of anguish and hospitals and treatments suffered by my beautiful daughter and shared by all who loved her."

He leaned back in his chair. The room was very quiet, dead. After a few seconds, he continued, "So 'something about my daughter' you ask, chief superintendent. Well, she was a golden girl, too good for this world. So brave, uncomplaining, happy even, no matter what shit life was heaping upon her poor little body.

She lost all her beautiful long flaxen curls, her skin became covered in painful sores, even her teeth fell out. Yes, her teeth—fell—out." His voice faded away, then he rallied, "The last thing she ever said, *smiling*, was 'Never mind, Daddy. I'm fine'. And then she died in my arms. She was sixteen."

Mike said, "My God, sir, how awful." His eyes were wet with tears.

"Thank you, detective inspector. I'm sorry to be so graphic. I still have not cried myself, I have—just died inside.

Anne, my wife died very shortly after Dawn died, she took her own life. She couldn't cope."

Len rose to his feet, massively. He stood for a moment, head bowed.

"I am so sorry. We will leave you in peace. We will not bother you again, sir."

At this moment the coffee arrived, carried by an elderly woman with a kindly face.

Selwyn said, "Please don't go. I'd love to talk to you about detective work. Tell me about Natalie Ellis. Sit down and have some coffee. Martha will be upset if you don't. She's my sister, you know. We live more or less by ourselves in this monstrosity of a house. Most of the old staff have retired or just left and we manage OK without them, don't we, sis?"

Len sat down again. They stayed for over an hour, swapping tales of detective work. Selwyn and Martha were both fans of crime stories and they had a great time. They both wished the two detectives every success in finding Natalie and returning her to her family, but Selwyn had never met the girl and the two coppers believed him absolutely. The day and time of the abduction he was able to detail and easily prove an alibi.

On the drive home, Len said, "What a lovely couple. No way are they suspects though, right, Mike?" Taff did not dare to ask his superior offices about the interview. Neither Mike nor Len felt capable of saying much beyond that.

Mike drawled, "I reckon." He grinned and they both chuckled. It relieved the tension. A bit. Taff just drove the car in silence. He was, on the whole, well pleased just to have been there with his two heroes.

Chapter Fourteen

Melissa rang her mum from the university, where she was in the final year of her BA (Honours) course in Nursing. She immediately sensed her mum, Jessica, was very upset about something.

"What is it, Mum, what's wrong?" She said sharply. She would brook no duplicity, she wanted the truth and she would have it. A very determined and capable young lady, Melissa.

"No dear, it's nothing really." But her voice sounded like she had been crying.

"Come on, Mum. I know something's happened. Tell me. You know you will and if you don't I'll go and get in my car now and come straight home. You know I will."

"Oh, Melissa darling. There's been another letter. I can't tell you about it on the phone, but don't come down tonight. Leave it to the weekend. I promise I'll tell you everything then. Your father wants to talk to you too."

"No way! Mum, I will be with you tonight. I'm only an hour away by car at this time of night. I'm ringing off now and I'll see you soon. Love you." She hung up grabbed a few things and within ten minutes she was on the road. She averaged 90mph along the motorway, overtaking BMWs, Jags and Mercs and never straying from the fast lane unless overtaking on the inside. She could be a very aggressive young lady when roused, Melissa!

She bounded into the house, shouting, "Mum, Mum, where are you, I'm home!"

Her mum was in the front lounge and she called out in reply. "Oh, Melissa, I'm in here with your dad."

They exchanged greetings, as Melissa, still bounding, came and hugged her parents.

Melissa wasted no time in coming to the point. "So you've had another letter. I want to see it. Where is it."

"Melissa, calm down, sit down, Jes, make us all some coffee with you while I talk to her?"

Melissa, for once, did as she was told. She sat down on a sofa, but held out her hand, saying firmly, "The letter, Dad."

"Hang on a minute, sweetheart. All in good time. Wait for your mother to join us. I'll tell you about the letter first." He went over to his daughter, knelt in front of her and held both of her hands, his eyes filling with tears. He gasped, "There's no easy way to say this, darling, according to the letter your beautiful sister is dead."

Melissa stared at him, her eyes popping wide open as the colour went out of her face. Her lips trembled and her mouth half-opened in a grimace of pain. "N—no, no you're lying, it's not true, it's not true, I don't believe you."

She beat at her father's chest with both of her fists, tearing away from his hold. Then she collapsed on the floor and vomited on the carpet. He picked her up and held her closely and they both sobbed violently together. Jessica came in and joined them, clutching both husband and daughter and howling with grief.

After what seemed an age, they quietened down, separated and stood up. Jessica went into the kitchen and fetched kitchen roll, tearing off sheet after sheet which she placed over the vomit on the carpet. David went and fetched a glass of water for Melissa to sip. They did not speak.

Eventually, things calmed down enough for Melissa to hold out her hand again and croak, "The letter. I want to see it. Now!"

Her father fetched it and handed it to her without a word. Jessica attempted to clean the carpet, to keep busy. The smell of vomit was all-pervading.

Melissa, sitting now by herself, read the letter. Then she read it again. Her face was wooden, drained, white. The letter slipped from her fingers onto the floor. She said, "I need to be alone. I'm going to bed now. I need to think."

She picked up her glass of water and headed off to her room, leaving her mum and dad looking at each other, expressionless.

Melissa did not sleep. She lay on the top of her bed, staring into space but thinking furiously. She was livid with anger at this man who had killed her sister, that much she knew and it comforted her to some extent. She would kill this man. She would have her revenge. Whatever the cost. She would pursue him to the ends of the earth if needs be. But how? How? She was just a young girl, powerless.

All these thoughts went round and round in her fevered brain. Then she thought about the gold. She would use it to fund her revenge! That was it! If it took her whole lifetime and her every penny she would exact her revenge. Her fists clenched she beat her pillow for a long, long time. Moaning.

Eventually, exhausted, she fell into a dreamless sleep.

In the morning she collared her dad before he set off to work. In fact, he was intending to stay at home that morning in any case in the light of last night's trauma. He too and his wife had had little sleep.

Melissa came straight to the point. "Did you get that money, Dad?"

"Yes, love, it is in six sacks of gold coins on the top of my wardrobe. Would you like to see it?"

"No!"

"Alright."

"Have you shown the police that letter?"

"Not yet, love. We are thinking about it, whether it would be of any use."

"How do you mean?"

"I don't know how with police would view that money, they may take it away as evidence or something."

"I see. Well, that is something I would like to talk to you about, Dad. I have an idea."

Part Three
Melissa

Chapter One

It was the morning briefing at the station. Superintendent Rowles opened the meeting, welcoming Dr Valentine, Rudi, as a visitor. Applause followed from the assembled team.

He said, "I would like to start off with a report about our inquiries into the missing schoolgirl, Natalie Ellis. Inspector Carter, Constable Parry and I have visited and questioned one of suspects, which we designated at the last meeting as being our prime suspect, Mr Selwyn Plant of Plant Homes Ltd. As Taffy reported to us last time, Mr Plant, a multi-millionaire, has recently lost a daughter of a similar age as the missing girl we are seeking.

I am sorry to have to report that in our opinion Mr Plant is no longer a suspect. In a very emotional meeting, we established beyond doubt that Mr Plant is totally innocent of any involvement. He is a lovely man sadly grieving a remarkable, brave and beautiful daughter and we have nothing but sympathy for him in this tragic case."

He paused, gulped some water and blew his nose noisily. The team were deathly silent. He continued, "I will now ask Rudi to report on his visit to another of the suspects. Rudi." Rudi flashed one of his room-illuminating smiles. There was a smattering of half-embarrassed applause. Many of the team were star-struck by this man.

"Hiya Folks. I love being over here in your lovely country—I don't think you really appreciate what you've got over here. But I must cut to the quick. The report I'm going to give is very much also the report of Penny over there. She really is a great young copper and going places fast—I'm real sure you all appreciate this fine detective, as I certainly do. Y'know, she was the one that that pointed in the direction of this guy we visited."

More applause and those close to Penny turned towards her and one or two patted her on the back. She was scarlet with pleasure and somewhat embarrassed. Rudi grinned at her. She was furious!

He continued, "Right! Well folks I reckon we have a new prime suspect in Dr Simon Shaw, the guy Penny and I went to interview. I am in the process of writing a profile of Simon. My gut reaction is that **he is the one we are looking for, I really do.**"

He paused, for effect. The atmosphere became electric. "He lives, on his own as far as we can tell, in a huge Victorian redbrick mansion deep in the heart of the country, well away from any other habitation, which is rare in this country except for the great houses of the nobility. He is rattling around in this weird house and he is a weird character to go with it. Not that we got to see the inside of the house, I must tell you, he gave us no chance of doing that, no sir!

We really have no idea of what it is like in the interior. All we were allowed to see was the long, winding drive, through tall hedges, to the house, a quick look at the front and the side and the back, where we sat on a terrace at the rear, in front of a massive conservatory, with slatted blinds closed, so again we saw nothing. The grounds are obviously very extensive but all we saw was a long and wide lawn down to some tall poplar-type trees a good distance away, hiding any view behind them.

Now this Simon is a charmer and he turned on the charm for us and answered all our questions graciously enough, but, as a psychiatrist I sensed very strongly that underneath all the charm he is a very damaged and dangerous personality, I've seen many similar guys in the past, charming and courteous, but hiding a beast inside of them. It shows if you know the signs, really guys.

He was really worried and frightened when I asked for a quick tour of the house and grounds and refused point blank. Penny will tell you we have no legal way to enforce a viewing or search of his property without a judge giving permission, a court order I think you call it and we have no chance at all of this happening.

This guy is super rich and has friends in high places and we have no evidence, only what would be reckoned as vague suspicions based on very weak grounds, that he may have known Natalie as a member of the school orchestra, for which he was an advisor and guest conductor and the fact that it was through Natalie's musical talents, as you all know, she was abducted."

Rudi paused and had a drink of water. He looked around the room. Gave another smile, then continued, "Another factor is his mother. I've done some digging around. I'd like to tell you folks something about his mother, Maggie Shaw. From an ancient family, loaded to the eyeballs, she was something else, this dame. A beautiful, wild, talented and hugely extrovert lady who was the leading light among the great and good of the county.

Her parties at her house, which is in the grounds of Simon's estate and in a fabulous Roman-style baths cum leisure centre, also on the grounds, were legendary. The guests, musicians, actors, judges, MP's, artists, all the so-called cultural icons of the country came to those parties, many of them naturists, as the Romans, naked, both sexes, champagne, but—amazingly—no sex allowed!

She also had a fully equipped concert hall attached to her ultra-modern home where she gave piano recitals and put on concerts with established artists and orchestras. Garden picnics, concerts, top-notch catering, the lot, folks. Like a midlands Glastonbury equivalent y'know?

Now and this is important, this lady died recently, an accident in the middle of the night, roaring at 100 mph on the M6 she crashed and died. Simon was obsessed with his mother. He never knew his father, but that is another story. She looked so young, though in her forties, that most people thought Simon, who always accompanied her, was her husband, rather than her son.

I reckon this loss, of his precious and hallowed mother is the root cause of his abducting young females. Not replacing a daughter, but a mother, however odd that might sound. He probably would not want to abduct another 40-year-old woman, as no one could compare with Maggie Shaw in any way, shape or form. No, he wanted to groom and nurture a replacement over many years, using a young and unformed girl as a model. That is my reasoning, folks, now—any questions?"

Complete silence followed for what seemed like an age, as Rudi just smiled and smiled. Len came to his rescue.

He said, "Well, now you know what Mike and I know— and we both know how gobsmacked we were, too, so don't worry too much. It's an awful lot to take in in one bite. Let's leave it there for now. After all, there's more to do than this case of a missing schoolgirl so I suggest we move on to other cases also needing to be reported upon. Rudi and I will leave you now and leave you in the capable hands of Inspector Carter. Mike?"

The meeting moved on, but Mike did say that a select team would now concentrate on Simon Shaw and do a full investigation into the man and his background, this would include detectives Parry and Summers.

Chapter Two

The firm, 'B&I Detectives' Agency', established some five years previously, was situated on New Street, running as a main high street shopping venue. It occupied a ground-floor corner position, where a narrow side road ran through. It was decorated in dark blue and gold lettering, which gave an air of quality and respectability.

Actually, the colour scheme reflected the fact that the two private detectives who founded the firm were ex-Royal Navy officers, Ben McGuire and Ian Jones. Ben, whose real name was Lord Ben Hawke, was a multi-millionaire landowner who, invalided out of the Navy, had started the agency as a hobby, to 'pass the time' and to solve a little problem his family had at the time, in that his two nephews had been kidnapped by a Nigerian group and had paid up some four million pounds for their safe return—but that is another story.

Ben's best mate from the Navy, Ian Jones, had joined with Ben to create the agency—the two men were very close and had shared many dangerous missions while on active service together in the Special Boat Service, the maritime equivalent to the Army SAS. Both men had done some fifteen years' service for Queen and Country and had found it difficult to settle down to civilian life.

Being a PI had been a boyhood dream for Ben, brought up by fictional heroes on film, TV and books, like Sam Stone and many others. The reality had turned out to be very different, of course, but they had persevered and were now very experienced in the job and had established a very high reputation in the locality.

The third member of the team was Pat Jones, now married to Ian, who had started as a secretary and was still acting as a receptionist but was a fully-fledged member of the team in every respect. A very attractive and charismatic lady, loved by all. Both men were huge, well over six feet tall Ben sported a big black beard and was built like a tank, but Ian was slim and elegant in build. Both men were in their early forties, but Pat was ten years younger and a natural blue-eyed blonde.

It was to this firm that Melissa Ellis went to one morning, having told her parents of her grand plan to discover the killer of her sister, Natalie, spending, if necessary, every penny of the 'compensation' money donated by the killer. This morning's appointment was some weeks later than the day the gold bullion had been delivered to the stables owned by her mother.

Melissa had done some detective work herself and had found out that the prime suspect of the police was a Dr Prof. Simon Shaw and had also found out about Simon's obsession with the loss of his mother, the impossibly glamorous Maggie Shaw. Searching far and wide she had discovered a private detective named Pat Jones, who might fit the grand plan she had been dreaming about since discovering that her sister had been murdered.

The appointment was for 11 am on a Monday morning. Receptionist Pat welcomed Melissa and asked her to take a seat in the waiting room while she informed Ben and Ian of her arrival. Melissa had dressed in a smart business suit for the meeting and looked quite attractive. She had lost weight and her teenage acne had virtually disappeared. Melissa had looked searchingly at Pat, rather to that young lady's surprise, it was usually the men who looked at her so intently!

Melissa said, "I assume you are Mrs Jones, one of the private detectives yourself—if you don't mind me enquiring?"

"Ah, so you have done some research into our agency, Miss Ellis! Yes, I am the receptionist, but I am also an experienced detective and as equally qualified as my husband, Mr Jones and our leader, Mr McGuire."

"I would like you to be present in the meeting then, please, Mrs Jones."

"Certainly. If you will just wait a minute, while I go and see the two men and then I will call you in and we can have a chat together, Alright?"

"Fine."

Seconds later, the four were comfortably ensconced in the rather plain but well-appointed office.

Ben, dressed in open-necked white shirt and black trousers, smiled genially at the young lady's prospective client. He said, "Ms Ellis. Welcome. Now, how can we help?"

Melissa got a file out of her shoulder bag and drew out a photograph, a newspaper cutting. She said, "This is a photograph of Dr Simon Shaw, a consultant plastic surgeon. The police believe, as I do, that he abducted and then murdered my sister Natalie. I want you to help me unmask this man and bring him to justice. I have here a folder of the work I have done and I have a plan in mind that might succeed, over time, possibly a long time, but I will never rest until that man receives justice for his crime."

"Wow, that's quite an opening statement, Ms Ellis!" exclaimed Ben, his black bushy eyebrows shooting up high into his mass of curly black hair. He passed the photograph to Pat, who looked at it carefully before passing it on in turn to her husband, Ian, who whistled thoughtfully.

Ian said, "Isn't he the so-called hero from the NHS who nearly died of Covid-19 last year, he was a much-admired man according to both the press and the TV, as I recall?"

Melissa said, "Yes, Mr Jones, that's the guy, although I believe he never went near the Covid patients, according to one of his colleagues."

Pat said, "Oh yes, I remember him. Very handsome young man I thought at the time."

"Oh yes, he's a handsome man, full of charm and a billionaire, largely inherited from his family," Melissa commented grimly.

"Wow!" said Ben, repeating himself. Not a great talker, Ben, more a man of action, in which he was awesome, being 6 foot 6 inches tall and eighteen stone of muscle, with a terrifying big black beard and fierce, piercing eyes.

One of his ancestors was a much-feared pirate who made a fortune from capturing Spanish treasure ships. He had sold the captured ships and the crews but kept what he could of the treasure. Ben was a decisive and powerful leader of the team, but he left most of the brain-work to Pat and Ian.

Pat said, "You said the police think this man abducted and killed your sister?"

"Yes. He is their prime suspect."

"So why are coming to us? Haven't you confident in the police inquiries?"

"It's not that. Simon Shaw is rich, a leading light in the county, with friends in high places. The police have no evidence and only have rather weak allegations and assumptions to go on. Dr Shaw lives in a vast mansion on his massive estate on the border of Shropshire. The police can do nothing in the way of searching his property or arresting him and questioning him. No judge would allow it.

You people, I imagine, have ways and means not open to the police so that is why I am coming to you to help me. I must be involved personally in this. Money is no object as my family was paid one million pounds by this man in return for Natalie, my sister."

Ian said, "Wow!" he couldn't help himself. He added, "Natalie—now are we talking about that schoolgirl who disappeared some weeks ago, reported widely in the media. Natalie *Ellis!* Of course. This was quite a famous news item. But you say, 'murdered'—how do you know she is dead? I don't remember this being reported."

"I can't tell you that. You'll have to take my word about it."

Pat raised both her hands and said, "No, you must tell us everything. It is vitally important and we cannot take on a case without that understanding."

Ben and Ian nodded.

"Can we discuss this at another time? I will have to think about it and there are others I need to think about."

"OK, but eventually we will need to know."

"Will you help me or not?"

Pat, who seemed to have taken over the lead, glanced at her two partners and they both nodded their heads for her to continue.

She said, "Well, tell us what you are planning, you say you have a plan in mind?"

Melissa started to answer, but Pat once again held up her hands. She said, "Look, let's have a coffee. We're not being very hospitable, Ms Ellis, sorry about that. I'll make us all a drink and find some biscuits and we can all think about what has been discussed so far."

Ian passed some company brochures and information about the agency to the young visitor to have a look at and she dutifully glanced through them while Pat operated the coffee machine and did the honours. They all settled down to their drinks and Ben and Ian munched biscuits happily. The ladies declined.

Melissa looked up and said, "I have decided that I can tell you why we know she has been murdered—we have had had a letter from the killer where he describes what happened. He said she attacked him and while defending himself he accidentally killed her."

Ben queried, "How do you know the letter is genuine?"

"There is no doubt. He has paid compensation, as I told you. Over one million pounds, in gold bullion. My father is a financial expert and runs his own company of financial advisors. He thinks the police will want to take away the gold as evidence. We want to use the money to fund the cost of obtaining justice for my sister and punishing this man."

"So the police have not seen this letter?"

"No, but this is the second letter. The police were given the first letter and it was useless in helping to find this man.

So, we reasoned, this second letter is unlikely to be of any use to them in unmasking the killer. Father knows the gold cannot be traced, so that is not an option either. Simon is obviously a very clever man and therefore very unlikely to leave any evidence to be found."

Ian asked, "Have you this letter, Ms Jones?"

"Call me Melissa, please—I can't stand 'Ms Jones!'—or just Mel, as everybody else does."

Ben grinned, "That's fine and I'm Ben, that's Ian and that's Pat, as you know. I'm all for first name use myself. Not one for formality, y'know."

Melissa grinned too. "Thank you, my Lord!"

Ben looked stunned. "Wow! You *have* been busy—are you thinking of being a PI yourself, then, Mel, it looks like you would be a good one!"

Mel replied, "In a manner of speaking, that's exactly what I'm doing, Ben—and actually you being of the aristocracy is partly why I have chosen your firm."

The three detectives looked startled at this revelation. Pat topped up their coffee cups. Two sugars each for the men. More biscuits were relished. By the men.

"Look," said the now pretty young visitor, "I'll tell you what my 'cunning plan' is if you like. Let me start by reading a copy of the abductor's letter to you and then I'll tell you about Simon's mother, Maggie and about the fantastic parties she used to host at their estate. Maggie Shaw was an amazing woman of incredible beauty and talent. This will take me a good half an hour, so stop me now if you don't want to be involved."

The three detectives, amazed at this remarkable girl's story, all nodded their heads vigorously. "Carry on!" they all said, almost in perfect sync and then they all laughed, including Mel. At the end of the meeting, no one was laughing.

Chapter Three

Simon was not a happy man at all. Following the visit of Rudi and Penny, he was, frankly, terrified. They said he was 'a person of interest'. All his plans for finding a replacement for Natalie were in tatters.

He had happily cut up Natalie's body into small pieces and fed them, one by one, into his septic tank, a necessity, as the remote estate was not connected to main drains. It was a huge tank, as befitted its task of coping with large amounts of foul water and solids when the parties and concerts were being held.

Simon, a trained surgeon, had no problem cutting up the young girl's body and managed to open an inspection hatch lid at the top of the tank, some 60 centimetres square, through which he dumped the body parts, one by one. The micro-biological action digested everything without a problem, of course. To all extent and purposes, Natalie no longer existed. The tank was in perfect balance and had not needed to be pumped out for years, though this remained an option.

He was worried that in the remote possibility of police searching his property for Natalie's body, they would have the septic tank pumped out and forensic science might detect that a body had been put in there. But, he reasoned, surely it would be impossible to prove it was Natalie's body. DNA of bone fragments, perhaps? Surely not. But he was not really sure and it worried him greatly. He could hardly ask for advice—

After Penny and Rudi had left, Simon had sat for hours staring into space, aghast at what had happened. Night came and he still sat there. He did not want to go to bed. Eventually, he dropped off to sleep where he sat, from exhaustion.

Morning came and he had to visit the nearest toilet. He thought about his poo and urine going into his septic tank, where the remains of Natalie were slowly being digested. This gave him some comfort. He loathed the girl for refusing to conform to his expectation. For ruining all his careful plans. After she had died, on the bed, he had beat her with his fists until his knuckles bled, in an uncontrollable rage.

Every day he raged at her memory. It was all her fault, not his. His plan was perfect. But now the thought of abducting another girl filled him with terror. "I am a person of interest, to the police. What did that mean?"

He asked himself this question ten times a day. Several times a police helicopter had flown low up and down his estate, for what seemed like hours. He had complained to the Chief Constable, a friend of his late mother and a frequent guest at her parties. The flights had stopped. But—were they looking for Natalie?

Despite his fears, in the weeks that followed Natalie's death, he had taken the gold bullion to the Ellis family, after a careful planning stage, where he watched her house and the stables. He went out most days and was sure he was not being followed. He noted that the Ellis mother and a friend took the horses out to exercise them every morning, leaving a Down's syndrome man in charge.

He knew enough about the Down's condition to risk taking the sacks of bullion himself, in his little white van. He had to pay the Ellis family the promised compensation to wipe away the guilt he felt. He wanted closure. His wife's family had invested in gold bullion ingots for over 100 years. They were kept in a secret impregnable underground vault in the basement of the Victorian mansion.

Maggie had carried on the tradition, buying gold coins and ingots, by a well-established circuitous route. She loved gold. Figures in statements did not excite her as gold did. Simon did not share her passion for gold and was glad to get rid of some. He knew it could never be traced, however, so it suited his purpose.

Time passed. He then felt he was going mad. It was the sense of isolation. He threw caution to the wind and returned to work at the hospital. They were hugely grateful and welcoming and it did help. He felt himself calming down. He tried to forget and just take each day as it came.

At work, he was soon his usual charming self, laughing and joking and behaving completely normally. He even began to wonder if he should return to Society, opening up his fabulous Roman baths leisure centre and inviting some of the old crowd. Why not? His mother would have been pleased, he was sure. The weeks passed without incident. He felt safe.

Chapter Four

Three Weeks Earlier

The police inquiry had stalled. Len had wangled some flights in a police helicopter over Simon's property and had received a furious phone call from the Chief Constable telling him in no uncertain terms that Dr Shaw was not to be bothered again, in any way, otherwise heads would roll!

Len, however, had taken a police photographer with him in the helicopter and they at least now had a good idea of the layout of the estate, both as still photographs and video footage. The team had been subjecting the images to extreme forensic examination, but so far with nothing useful achieved. No sign of disturbed earth, for example, where a body may have been buried.

Then, one morning, they had a telephone call from Melissa Ellis, requesting a meeting with "whoever was in charge of the case of the missing Natalie Ellis, her sister."

DI Mike Carter decided to meet the girl. He had, of course, met her on the occasion when he had gone to the Ellis home to see the letter the family had received allegedly from the abductor, offering compensation of one million pounds in return for Natalie.

Melissa had torn into him on the occasion, accusing him of being unconcerned about the safety of her sister and being light-hearted and casual in his attitude. He had been quite devastated at the time and was ashamed about his behaviour, which, in retrospect, he realised was stupid and unprofessional. He was not looking forward to meeting Melissa again but thought that he would use the opportunity to apologise to her.

So when the appointment time came, he met the young girl in his office and prepared himself for another ferocious attack. But Melissa actually just wanted information and she felt guilty about withholding evidence. The Ellis family had decided not to tell the police about the second letter or the gold and had agreed to her plan to make use of the money by using it to fund a private investigation into what now appeared to be Natalie's murder.

Her father had been secretly relieved that Melissa had not insisted that the letter and the money be immediately handed over to the police. He had thought that his daughter, who could be very strong and stroppy, might have ruined his ideas of investing the gold and making himself and the family very rich indeed. So he had readily agreed to Melissa's plan as a much better alternative.

He would control the finance, of course, as the expert in the family. He could not envisage the private detective work would cost much of the capital. But Melissa had not told her father everything! She had very big ideas in mind—

Melissa came straight to the point. "I have come for information. I intend to hire a firm of private detectives to investigate my sister's disappearance. Not because I do not trust the police are doing their best to find out what has happened to her, I'm very satisfied with the way particularly you, Inspector, have kept us informed about the progress of your inquiry. No, I am hiring a private detective firm to assist the police. I am aware that the police are handicapped by rules and regulations which are not such a barrier for private detectives."

Mike said, "I see. Well, of course, I can't stop you hiring a private detective but I would not advise this as a plan of action. I doubt very much they will have any better results than we have with all the modern resources at our command.

Our computer database is vast and very comprehensive and not available to private firms, of course, just as one example. Such things as fingerprints and DNA labs are another example not available elsewhere. But, if you are determined, of course, it is entirely up to you how you spend your money. I should think you will be facing very considerable costs, I must warn you."

"Yes, I have researched this very thoroughly, Inspector Carter, all you say is known to me, but the firm I have chosen, B&I Detective Agency, has some staff with special abilities able to go undercover, for example, to root out the culprit. I need to know the names of suspects, that is all I need from you. The information will be absolutely secure and guaranteed kept secret from the media. I will sign any disclosure agreement willingly."

Mike looked at the girl thoughtfully. He really wanted to nail Simon Shaw and it looked like he had no way to achieve this lawfully. He admired Melissa tremendously. Should he take a chance?

He said, "I am going to trust you, Ms Ellis. But this conversation never happened, is that clear?"

"Agreed!"

"I have good reason to name the person who abducted your sister as a Dr Simon Shaw, billionaire celebrity, but we are unable to investigate him, for political reasons. That is all I can offer you. You did not get this name from me, understand? I am breaking every rule in the book."

"I understand perfectly. Thank you from the bottom of my heart."

"Get that bastard. For me."

Mike was trembling with emotion from the enormity of what he had just done. If it ever came out, his career was over.

Chapter Five

Present Day

The Midsummer Masked Ball was in full swing. All the big names in the County were there, as always. Unfortunately, the weather was not living up to the name at all. It was cold, wet and windy, so all the elegantly dressed guests were indoors, but the fifteenth-century manor house was huge and managed to accommodate everyone with ease.

The Earl and Countess of Nevin, owners of the house, were doing their duty as hosts, trying to circulate among the hundred or so revellers. The fizz was flowing freely and much laughter and merriment rang out as they moved slowly from couple to couple.

John, the Earl, reached a youngish couple he did not recognise at once, a really stunning blonde in a gold dress and matching tiny mask which did little to disguise her beauty, with a very tall and heavily-set man bearing a big black jutting beard which made mask wearing difficult, so he just wore a rather jaunty eye-patch, such as his Pirate ancestor might have worn.

John's face cleared as he recognised the man. "Ben Hawke! My word! I haven't seen you for years. I would not have expected to see you among this lot anyway, not your scene, really, old darling? And, by Jove, where have you been hiding this amazing beauty, you old dog? Is it your wife? I know you got married to an Irish lady, daughter of some rock star or other, wasn't it? I say, I hope I haven't been speaking out of turn."

The Earl suddenly wondered if he committed an unwarranted gaffe. Far too much champers too early. He turned to the lady in some confusion, but she laughed musically.

The lady said, "Don't worry! You're right and Ben's wife was unable to come tonight, but I'm her friend, Maggie. I twisted his arm to bring me here. I know no one here. Come on Ben, you should be introducing me, you oaf!"

Ben bowed, "Maggie, allow me to introduce John, the Earl of Niven, for his sins."

Maggie gave a charming, if mocking, curtsy, continuing to laugh.

"Enchante!"

John took Maggie's arm and tucked it through his. He said, smiling broadly, "Look, your enormous escort is useless at this sort of thing. Come along with me, I'll have the great pleasure of escorting you, as the most gorgeous lady I've seen for many a long year. My dear, you are ravishing and I claim you for at least an hour."

"That's lovely. Thank you kindly, sir!"

As Ben gratefully melted into the background and headed for the food, John and Maggie, arms linked carried on circulating among the guests. It all went very well for about twenty minutes. Then, as they approached a small group of men, one of them suddenly cried out. He was a handsome thirty-something man, very elegantly dressed and wearing a full-face mask of an exotic bird.

Simon Shaw, for that, was who it was, at his first real outing in high society since the death of his mother. He seemed to stagger and looked as if he was going to faint. John went and put an arm around him.

He joked, "Hey, hey, brace up, young man! you look like the bubbly has gone to your head. Are you all right? Oh, it's Simon, isn't it, Simon Shaw? Come, let me introduce you to my gorgeous companion here, she'll cheer you up, man. Maggie, let me introduce Simon, he's a surgeon and a local hero—of the Covid pandemic thing. Thank heaven it all seems to be going away a bit now, otherwise we wouldn't be here tonight. Masks are a bit ironic, really, this year. We've all had enough of the devilish devices."

Simon stammered, "Did you say, 'Maggie'—I don't believe it!—I thought for a moment you were my mother, you are the image of her, when she was younger I suppose, but she always looked so young you know. Her name, her dress, her face, her hair, it's amazing, amazing—" his voice tailed off and again he seemed to be about to faint.

The Earl continued to hold him upright. He said, "I say, old boy, are you OK? I mean to say, you're a doctor, so well, I don't know what to do."

Maggie, who had remained silent so far, spoke. "Hello, Simon. I suppose I should be upset if I look like your mother, but that aside, it's nice to meet you. I assure you I'm no relative. I'm born and bred and live in Ireland and I'm only here visiting Ben Hawke, the Earl of Somerton, you know?

He's married to my friend who could not come tonight, so he brought me instead, otherwise I would not have been here at all. I'm sorry if I have upset you, but it really is just a coincidence if I look a little like your mother and I'm really sorry for your loss."

Simon, who had been staring at her all through this, seemed to be recovering his composure. "I know it's silly, but the lighting in here is so dim and the room is so hot and clammy. I'm fine really, I suppose I'm still grieving for my mother.

She was such an amazing woman, a truly beautiful person in every way imaginable. She and I were inseparable and had no need for anyone else. But, I mustn't bore you. Look, I must see you again. Really I must. At my place. Soon, before you disappear like Cinderella at the Ball." He laughed, a little too loudly for comfort.

"Ah well now, Dr Shaw, is it? I can see you could charm the birds from the trees and you quite possibly could charm me too, so I would be delighted to accept your invitation, my dear Prince Charming, but I'll leave my glass slippers at home if you don't mind!"

She laughed, then said in a sort of mock confidentiality, hand in front of her mouth, "It's the best offer I've had since I've been over here visiting stuffy old Ben, who I love to bits really. So ring me at Ben's and I'll come running!"

She thought to herself, "We're IN! That's exactly what Mel wanted, the first part of her 'cunning plan' has gone like clockwork. Clever girl, that!" The fact that she was planning to go alone to meet a probable murderer had not yet sunk in—

Pat had quite enjoyed playing the part of the dead mother of Simon. Weeks of preparation had gone into this: the study of many photographs, copying a favourite gold lame dress, a hairstyle, even her movements and carriage. All expenses covered by the Ellis fortune and the sum had been considerable already.

Mel had been involved at every step, she and Pat were by now firm friends. Pat would take Mel with her to Simon's, telling him it was her baby sister Dawn, who insisted on coming along too—Two girls would be in less danger, too, they said to Ben and Ian, who would be with the girls, secretly. They would have to get into Simon's estate somehow, despite all the alarm systems.

Ian was a gifted electronics expert, Royal Naval Intelligence trained, so that should not be too much of a problem, hopefully.

Chapter Six

The fire service was called to Dr Simon Shaw's house one night, following a report by a local farmer, who late in the afternoon had spotted a lot of smoke coming from the mansion, although it was hidden by trees, it was obvious where the smoke was coming from. There was a glow in the sky as night fell, too. The fire service had to use axes and sledgehammers to break down the gates to gain access. Alarms howled. It was pitch dark, lit only by the flames from the mansion. A fox kept howling, spookily.

The fire turned out to be extensive and spreading quickly. More fire engines were called for and it took several days before any of the firefighters could gain entrance. The Victorian builders had done their job well and the walls were still standing proud, but the roof had gone and the interior was ravaged by the fire and the water.

They found the owner dead, burnt to a cinder, in what little remained of his fabulous Victorian mansion. Forensics discovered a bullet in his head. He had evidently been the victim of a murder. The media were delighted, of course. Local hero doctor in his fabulous mansion, brutally murdered by person or persons unknown. Great storyline.

The Chief Constable had personally rung Detective Chief Superintendent Len Rowles at his home, lifting the embargo on investigating Dr Shaw, now that he was the victim of an outrageous crime. So it was that Len and Mike called a special meeting of the murder team and Len rang Rudi, inviting him back over from his USA homeland. Rudi had asked to be kept informed of any developments in the case of Natalie Ellis's disappearance.

DI Mike was seriously worried. This was the last thing he expected. He felt guilty and sick with dread that his helping Melissa Ellis might have turned into a tragic nightmare. For him. And his family. He did not know what to do. Had Melissa shot Simon? It was a possibility. The girl was obsessed with revenge for the death of her sister. He knew that for a fact.

He also knew she was strong and determined and would stop at nothing or no one to achieve what she wanted. He knew he could never confess to his boss or anyone really, the stupid thing he had done, as he regarded it now. If it had led to the murder of Simon Shaw, whether or not he had killed Natalie, could never be condoned, he thought grimly.

He would have to just sit tight and say nothing. Nothing else to do. He knew it would weigh heavily on his conscience the rest of his days.

He attended the meeting with a heavy heart. Len asked him to address the team and bring them up to date with the murder of Dr Shaw, which would now have to be a number one priority.

Mike stood at the front, with a new screen, on which was pinned a recent photograph of Dr Shaw, taken from a newspaper cutting at the time he was hot news having survived Covid-19.

He said, "A new case for us and one I must admit I find very difficult. As you all know, Dr Shaw, seen here, was our prime suspect in the case of the missing schoolgirl Natalie Ellis and the previous case of the missing schoolgirl Kylie Thomas. If you recall, Rudi and Penny went to interview him and following that interview, Rudi told us that it was his opinion that Dr Shaw was very probably the abductor both of Kylie and of Natalie.

We all know and respect Rudi's opinion, of course, he is probably the world's finest expert in the field of psychological detection of crime. So we might say to ourselves if someone has murdered Dr Shaw, well and good, he deserved to be brought to justice one way or another."

There were murmurs of agreement with this last point. Mike held up both his hands, "Yes, that's probably the sort of thing we may be thinking, as I am, but we must guard against this, as professional detectives. We are here to dispense justice, yes, but only by lawful means, observing the best traditions of the British Justice System in that no person is found guilty of a crime unless he has had a fair trial and every opportunity to defend himself in a court of law.

We may be sure in our own minds about a person's guilt, but that's not enough. We must gather evidence and prove beyond doubt every case we investigate. Human Rights are inviolate. In the case of Kylie, it is known she died of an asthma attack aggravated by Covid-19. In the case of Natalie, we do not know whether she is alive or dead, although we rather suspect that she is probably dead. We were unable to investigate further our prime suspect because of pressure from on high. You all know what I mean by that and I am not going to say any more on that topic."

There was an undercurrent of growls of dissent at this statement, but no one had the courage to stand up and be counted.

"So the question is, 'who shot Dr Shaw?' I, personally, haven't a clue! But that is why we're having this meeting. Put your thinking caps on and let's have some suggestions. Please!" His face was, very unusually, pale, grim and tired-looking.

Sergeant Phipps (known as 'Phippy') stood up. "What about the fire then, sir? The place was burnt to the ground wasn't it, sir?" He pronounced the word 'fire' as 'foyer'. The unique black country accent, of course.

"Well, not to the ground, the builders were good in those days, some walls are still standing proud. But yes! You're right, Phippy, it's another question and again we are not too sure about whether it was arson or something else. The fire service did not find evidence of an accelerant having been used or any obvious electrical fault, etc, so it is another mystery I'm sorry to say."

DC Ivor Parry (Taff) stood up and said, "Can forensics tell us about the weapon used on Dr Shaw and was he dead before the fire started or what, sir?"

"Apart from the fact that it was a standard 9mm bullet fired at close range from a pistol of some kind, no. No weapon has been found at the scene. As for the second part of your excellent question, Taff, Dr Shaw was definitely dead before the fire started."

Penny asked, "Sir, when Rudi and I visited the mansion we noted that the security on the place was extensive and looked very difficult to bypass. I imagine the notion of a burglar or other intruder gaining access and perpetrating this murder is very much a non-starter. So I would think whoever did the deed was there by invitation and was someone known to Dr Shaw?"

"Yes, thanks, Penny. A good point. We have found out that the doctor had recently gone back to work and also that he had attended the Masked Ball given by the Earl and Countess Nevin, which is normally an annual charitable event given in aid of local hospices.

Many of the county's great and good were in attendance for the first time in three years, including the chief constable, now that the Covid-19 regs have been eased. We are not sure, but we believe that at that event a certain glamorous lady was seen talking with Simon Shaw in an intimate manner and we are at present investigating this story, which looks promising. Apparently, she was the image of his late, lamented mother."

Penny asked, "Do we have a name for this 'glamorous' lady, sir?"

"Yes, detective, it was, let me see, a Maggie LeBon, a guest of the Earl of Somerton, Lord Ben Hawke, who, believe it or not, owns a private detective agency in Lancashire! This may be significant. We, at the moment, know nothing of this lady friend of the Earl and he is not giving us much information except that she was an old school friend of his wife, the Countess, visiting for a few days. They were both at Dublin University too, apparently.

The Countess told us that Maggie had phoned her out of the blue and that she had not seen her in years. This unexpected visitor, according to the Earl, is no longer in this country but has gone travelling in Africa. He, nor his wife, knew how to contact her in any way. So, she is a bit of a mystery, I'm sorry to say. Of course, she is a person of interest in this case.

Maggie was the name of Simon's dead mother and we know Simon was obsessed with his mother and devasted by her demise. So we will continue to try to locate her, but it doesn't look easy. These are all very rich, powerful aristocratic people. You all know the score. Don't hold your breath!"

"Wow!" "Gosh" were the general comments from the team.

Chief Superintendent Len Rowles stepped in and said, "I think we'll leave that one there, for now, team. Return to your duties." He was grinning.

He was looking forward to seeing his close friend, Rudi, who had promised to come as soon as he could manage it, now that there were developments in the Natalie abduction case. This was promising to be a case even Sherlock Holmes himself would have found intriguing! He was loving every minute of it and couldn't wait to discuss it with his old friend, over a good dinner and a few whiskies.

Chapter Seven

Rudi duly arrived and took a taxi to Len's large house in Solihull, a suburb of Birmingham. He had the pleasure of being instantly covered with Len's five cats all determined to lick his face as he lay on his back with his feet in the air, laughing uproariously. He looked so much better than the last time he had visited the superintendent. He still missed his wife and baby son every minute of each day, but he was able to push such needs to the back of his mind a little more than the last time.

There were times of complete anguish, of course, but they were becoming easier to handle. A little at a time. He loved visiting Len. He loved England. He loved having a crime to solve and this abduction case was a real humdinger of a problem. He was keeping a diary of the case and hoped to make a book about the psychological drama evolving in Wolverhampton's fair city region.

Despite jetlag from the long journey, Rudi managed to enjoy his first evening chatting with his host and managed to stay awake until midnight, after a good meal beautifully cooked by the massive chief super, who was a keen cook and watched all the cookery programmes on the TV, of which there were legion!

They did not discuss the Natalie case at all the first night and when Rudi finally dragged himself off to his pleasant bedroom, he went instantly to a dreamless sleep with three of the soft, velvety, small warm bodies of Len's cats sharing his extra king-sized bed. He now could identify the three with ease, they were 'two, three and five', whereas 'one and four' slept with their owner. All perfect British Blues.

Three was a snorer, at times loud and rasping, but she failed to keep the jetlagged visitor awake for a minute! All five were neutered queens and thus there was never any fighting between them. A set of perfect pussy pets and nothing was spared to make their lives as luxurious as any pussy's heart could desire.

All the latent love that was deep inside the massive superintendent was lavished on his five precious pets, for Len was unable to have a normal relationship with a human being due to his father's sexual abuse of his beloved older sister leading to her suicide at the age of 16 and to a complete mental breakdown for himself, resulting in years in a mental institution and a permanent abhorrence of being touched by anyone.

It was against this background that Len settled down with his closest-ever friend Rudi and started to tell him about the saga of the abductions carried out by Dr Prof. Stephen Shaw.

As both were fans of the stories about the fictional great detective of 14B Baker Street, London, Sherlock Holmes, with his trusty companion Dr Watson, Len had tried to recreate the stories' atmosphere in his lounge, with low lighting and a flickering fire, albeit a fake electronic version! His notion was of himself as Watson, of course, rather than as Sherlock, which he assigned to his friend.

When the two friends were comfortably seated, Len said that he would give a brief summary of the abduction case from the beginning, ignoring the fact that Rudi knew much of story already, as a means of refreshing his memory.

He started, "A really curious case, this, Holmes old chap, as I think you will agree. Two innocent young girls abducted at different times over a period of eighteen months or so. The first resulting in the death of the child concerned, Kylie Thomas, but strangely, death by natural causes and the second where the fate of the other girl, Natalie Ellis is as yet unresolved, but she is probably dead, murdered one may assume."

He paused and Rudi intoned, "Go on, my dear Watson!" His English accent was, frankly, appalling, thus all the more amusing.

"Indeed, Holmes. As far as the Thomas case goes, we have no real leads. We have been quite unable to find any evidence and we honestly did not have a clue where to go next. The Ellis girl, though, was very different."

"Ah, the letter—yes, of course."

"Indeed," repeated his host. "As you say, the letter. Written almost certainly by the perpetrator and offering one million pounds as compensation for the loss of their daughter, Natalie. This letter has been subjected to the most extensive of forensic tests, but, alas and alack! I fear with no useful results.

But this letter, assuming it was from the abductor did allow us to make some assumptions of value, in that the perpetrator must be very rich, in order to be able to afford the promise made. Added to that was the method used to lure the young lady into his spider's web.

Another letter, purporting to be from her school, inviting Natalie to a masterclass on the oboe, an instrument that she plays in the school orchestra. This sent the girl off on her bike to the school—a journey from which she did not return. A journey that without doubt resulted in her abduction and capture. The masterclass, of course, did not really occur."

Len paused, a took a long draught of his favourite whiskey, which he drank with an equal measure of Malvern water. Rudi grinned and joined him. He was drinking Jack Daniels' bourbon whisky, as he had brought a case over with him of his preferred tipple.

Len continued. "Our murder squad had identified some rich persons, all of them connected with Natalie's school. The abductor must have had good knowledge of the girl to have written the letter, on genuine school notepaper, to know she played oboe in the school orchestra and to know she generally went to the school on her bicycle.

Among the possibles identified by the team, in the form of Detective Constable Penny Summers, was a certain Dr Prof. Simon Shaw, who, as you know, was chairman of the school governors, a musical advisor to the school orchestra, which he, on occasion, conducted. Simon Shaw was a gifted musician and competent ballet dancer.

He was well known in the County for his musical abilities. His mother and he organised regular performances, of Operas and Ballets, at their Estate which was a sort of Midlands equivalent of Glyndebourne. The Shaw family goes back centuries and has amassed a huge fortune. Their estate, I have heard, from the chief constable, often a guest, was something to behold—really fabulous."

"His mother is the key to the whole case, I believe, Len," observed Rudi, nodding his head, sagely. He made as if he was playing a violin, grinning broadly at the same time. The two men enjoyed a chuckle—and another swallow of whisky to follow.

Len said, "Yes, Simon was obsessed, it appears, with his mother, who everybody says was an incredibly gorgeous lady, immensely cultured and talented and a huge loss to the social life of the county. Many people thought Maggie was the wife of Simon on first meeting, as she was so young-looking and it was obvious that the two adored each other. But it was a mother/son relationship of course, which is common enough. Freudian implications, as I know you will be very familiar with, Rudi."

"Ah, the Oedipus Complex raises its' ugly head again, old friend. But actually, that is really a childhood condition according to Sigmund, where a child loves his mother and hates his father, seeing him as competition for her love. The Greek tragedy where the king unknowingly marries his mother causing her, when she finds this out, to commit suicide and him putting out his own eyes—is something very different of course.

I very much doubt there was any sexual desire between Simon and his mother, to me they were both narcissistic and were in love with themselves as much as each other. Simon was totally obsessed with his mother and they both were completely dependent on each other.

After Maggie died, Simon could not cope with life. He became mentally disturbed—insane, to be frank. This led to him abducting children, thinking he could mould one into taking his mother's place in his life. A fascinating case.

There's a book in this for me, Len!" Len nodded his head, sagely.

The two men said nothing for a while, each busy with their own thoughts. Then Len sat up straight and said, "Look, Rudi, would you like to come with me tomorrow to Simon Shaw's home, which is still a crime scene. I know you and Penny have already been to the estate and I have been also since the murder of Simon, of course, but I think you might value a look at what remains of the inside of the Victorian Pile, it really was a remarkable house, as you will see. We have to somehow discover Simon's killer and this time we have the full backing of those on high!"

"The game's afoot!" they both shouted, laughing uproariously. Several more whiskies late, the two men staggered up to their rooms, followed by all the cats, good companions to the last.

Chapter Eight

The next morning the two men, freshly showered but somewhat bleary-eyed, greeted each other in the large country-style 18 foot square kitchen. Being a keen cook, Len kept his kitchen pristine and it looked very attractive in the morning sunlight, copper pans gleaming on the tiled walls.

It had a central large scrubbed-top oak table and it was there where the two men sat to eat a traditional Full English Breakfast. Rudi had now really got a taste for English sausages and he tucked in with relish, foregoing the maple syrup-covered pancakes that were his custom over the Pond.

The cats, all five of them, came sleekly in through the cat flap, having been doing their duties outside somewhere. Somewhere that Len did not know, oddly, but he suspected they visited a piece of common wooded land that was just over the road. No doubt they spent much of the night hunting wood mice. There were two large litter trays provided, but it was rare that they were used. Fortunately, they never brought any trophies home with them!

The five cats began a cats' chorus of purrs and meows and rubbing their softly furred little bodies against the two men's legs. Len, who had finished his breakfast, gave up the struggle and went to feed them their mixture of canned and packeted cat foods. Tails in the air the cats soon finished them off. Each had its' own bowl, of course.

There were also some bowls of water provided and as they drank their tails gradually descended. Rudi labelled this phenonium as their *tailometers!* He asked Len if he ever gave them milk, but he was told this was always a disaster as much as they loved milk it always made them sick. So the answer was firmly in the negative on that one.

Len loaded the dishwasher and shortly afterwards they got in his car, a black Jaguar, to set off to visit Simon Shaw's estate on the Shropshire border, a journey of at least an hour's duration. Len quite enjoyed pointing out the various highlights of the route. Then Rudi turned to the subject in hand.

He said, "Say, Len, as you know, the clearest and most common motive for a murder is always financial. So, in the light of this, do you know who is likely to inherit what appears to be a vast fortune tied up in the Shaw family. Tell me, if you know, something about this before we arrive, perhaps?"

Len grinned. "Ah, yes, I have been doing a fair bit of research on that topic, Rudi. I intended to fill you in on this last night, but somehow we didn't get around it and the whisky flowed and the company was great, so I forgot."

"Sure thing. Yes, Len, it was a really good night. I am forever in your debt for rescuing me from myself and making my life seem tolerable again to some extent. Coming over here to old England and to you and your cats—I really can't tell you how you've helped me, old friend."

Len cleared his throat noisily.

After a few moments, he continued. "So, the Shaw estate. As you say, Rudi, there's a huge fortune waiting for somebody which must be the most obvious reason why he has been murdered. I'll tell you all I know, but it isn't a lot. For a start, as far as I can make out Simon did not leave a will. This is quite understandable.

It is not long really since his mother died, still quite young and fit and Simon was a young man—a young, very troubled man—he just did not get around to making a will, according to the very top-notch firm of lawyers that the family used. His mother also had not made a will. The lawyers told me that Simon was the last known member of the Shaw family. His mother was a single child, as was Simon, so there's no obvious candidate to inherit the estate. The Shaw family has simply died out. Completely."

"Wow!" said Rudi. "I don't know anything about British Law. I wonder what will happen?"

"If no credible person can be found to inherit, eventually the entire estate will revert to the Crown, apparently, Rudi! Until the lawyers give out their verdict. We can't touch the estate and it could take years. At present they are about to do a search to make sure there are no living relatives that might have a claim—when they get around to it—and you know what lawyers are like the world over."

"Wow!" repeated the passenger. "So that's not a motive, for sure. Whoever shot the guy just wanted to kill him dead and that's all there was to it. That's certainly narrows the field, Len! Revenge rears its' ugly head again."

They were silent for the rest of the journey, which was a matter of only a few minutes before they arrived at the gates. A lone constable was on duty and he examined Len's credentials, saluted smartly and let the pair inside. The long drive completed, they arrived at the house. Police teams were still active in the building but on that morning there was nobody about, so the two friends entered through what remained of the front entrance. The place was absolutely chaotic and smelt foul. Rubble everywhere, charred remnants of wood and fabric were strewn about in heaps, where the forensics had been searching.

Len knew where the body had been found, as he had been one of the first at the scene, so they picked their way through the debris to find the familiar chalk outline of Simon Shaw's body, where what was left of it had been found, in the manner of all bodies that had been burnt, with his fleshless arms stretched out in front of his chest as if he was having a fight. Of course, there was no body now to be seen, only the pathetic chalk outline.

The two men said nothing for a while. Len thought Rudi would like to soak up the general atmosphere. The American just stood there for a few minutes and bent his head as if in prayer; then he looked at his friend. His face was very sad looking.

Rudi said, "Hey, what a mess! Look, there's nothing more to be gained here as far as I can see, but I sure appreciate you bringing me here. When Penny and I interviewed the young man, I thought he was a fine specimen of manhood, well made, fit and strong, highly intelligent, cultured in the extreme, but battling with mental trauma. This awful place and the chalk outline is all that is left of what was, in essence, a very tragic story. I would like to see more of the house and the grounds now, please. If the lawyers allow it.

Fine. Let's do that. I was lucky enough to come here with Ken Platt, that's Sir Kenneth Platt, the Chief Constable. A pleasant companion as it happens and very good at his job. He knows this place very well as he was an old friend of Maggie Shaw and a regular visitor at the concerts, the operas, etc, plus enjoying the amazing leisure facilities this place has got. He was quite devastated looking around. But he gave me a lot of useful information.

Look, we can walk over to the private leisure centre shortly, although it has been all boarded up now. But first, let me show you the fabulous mirrored ballroom in the East Wing of his mansion. It almost escaped the fire completely. Very little damage. Come along, Rudi, you will be amazed. I certainly was.

Have you been to Versailles? It's a perfect copy of the mirrored ballroom there, would you believe. It's such a good thing that it wasn't destroyed by the fire. The Fire Service did an excellent job, as always."

"They sure did. No, sir, I've never been to Versailles, France, but I've always wanted to. The opportunity has never happened."

"Amazing place. Amazing gardens. Astonishing fountains. Superb. You must go. It's a 'must see' place, Rudi. I'll come with you if you like."

"It's a date!" They both laughed, relieving the tension, as they picked their way gingerly back to entrance hall. The smell was appalling even though both men were wearing Covid masks.

Rudi remarked as they walked, "The elephant in the room, of course, is the question of the whereabouts of Natalie Ellis. I imagine you have been searching for any sign of her abduction in the house and the grounds?"

"Yes, of course, Rudi. But as far as this house is concerned there are a lot of questions. For example, we think that a house of this size and age would certainly have had extensive cellars but, if so, they are filled with hundreds of tons of rubble where the roof and the floors and some of the internal walls have collapsed and fallen.

It would take a tremendous amount of work to clear all the debris out of the way in order to search any cellars there may be down below us. We were really lucky to have found Simon's body—the odds were totally against us finding anything in that part of the house. A small part of the concrete ceiling had remained in place leaving a gap in the rubble just where his body happened to be.

We think it was in one of the reception rooms on the far side of the house, leading on to the conservatory. This is where we have just been. As you will have seen, all around us is totally piled with rubble. But we have been assured it was safe for us to go and see where the body was found. We have to thank the fact that at some time in the past a reinforced concrete ceiling had been installed in that part of the house so that the rooms above could be converted into a gymnasium."

"I see. But what about the grounds and any other buildings, no luck there I imagine?"

"Nothing found at all. The grounds and the other buildings have all been searched thoroughly and a full forensic examination for fingerprints, fibres, DNA, you name it. Nothing."

"Good news, anyway! If rather unexpected. Where on earth is Natalie? Any ideas, Len? Do you think she is alive or dead?"

"God knows," said the superintendent, gloomily. "Vanished off the face of the Earth. The only place we haven't searched is the septic tank, but if she is in *there* we couldn't identify it according to the experts—and would you like to tell a grieving mother that her daughter was in such a place? Better not to know than that, I would think."

"Surely she's not there, Len—that's awful, monstrous, no, you can't be right." Rudi looked and sounded horrified at the thought. "I can't see that guy we met doing something as evil as that."

"I'm sure you're right. But, *if* she is dead, she could be anywhere. On average very few bodies are found where the murderer has had time to dispose of the body. The ones found by dogs on their walkies are badly hidden and easy for animals to dig up. Lord knows how many are buried at sea or in lakes and rivers, suitably weighted down. There was a case recently in Ireland where the murderer was in charge of a crematorium!"

"I don't believe it!"

Len laughed. "Only joking, Rudi!"

By this time the two men had arrived at the magnificent mirrored ballroom which was virtually unharmed and had its own entrance. They both stood in awe looking at the fantastic room, which, even without the crystal chandeliers lit, was an incredible sight.

A vast room highly decorative with a beautiful plasterwork ceiling and a long line of huge chandeliers. The walls had full-length windows down both sides interspersed with similar size massive mirrors. For anyone dancing on the floor between the mirrors, of course, the effect was magical as the reflections seemed to go on and on into a spatial infinity time after time after time.

Lit by hundreds of candles at night, with the music playing and the dancers swirling around dressed in all their finery—jewels sparkling on swelling bosoms, coat-tails flying—just breath-taking!

Len said, "Apparently this was not used very often except by Simon and his mother practising ballet dancing with their master. But I imagine in the nineteenth century the scene would have been wonderful on the evenings when all the ladies and the gentleman were dancing, perhaps to a Strauss waltz. What do you think, Rudi."

"Wow! You old Romantic, Len! Make a good film set for a Jane Austen film though!" he laughed and punched his friend playfully on the shoulder. He added, musing, "I must have a word with Stephen when I go home." Len tried not to shudder at being touched.

He said, "Stephen?"

"Spielberg, y'know."

"What? You know Stephen Spielberg?"

"Just kidding, Len!"

"Touché, mon ami!"

Len, chuckling, announced, "Come on, I'll show you the main wonder of the estate next. Sir Ken was waxing lyrical about it. It is really fantastic—just across the lawn is a line of poplars hiding another world. Come and see! Stretch your legs!" he started off at a good pace across the vast lawn.

And, indeed, as the two men cut through the poplars, the landscape opened out in front of them. A very extensive lake lay ahead, looking rather beautiful, very naturalised with reeds and bullrushes, iris, water lilies, all in profusion. On the left of the lake, set back, was a very modern-looking house, long and low, with sweeping overhanging roofs.

But to the right of the lake was an amazing building, which at first glance looked like something one would find in

Rome. A vast stone edifice, surrounded by columns and pediments looking like a Roman Baths might have looked two millennia in the past. To add to the beauty of the scene were the lovely Shropshire hills as a background.

Rudi gasped. Len chuckled, a deep rumbling sound.

"Fantastic, eh?"

"Sure is, Len. What is it, then? A film set?"

"In fact, so the chief constable was telling me, it is a private leisure centre in the style of a Roman Baths, but subtly updated. It basically was a sort of mixture of Turkish Baths and a modern Sauna. Apparently, two or three times a year Maggie Shaw hosted a sort of Bacchanalian Roman Festival here.

Both Maggie and Simon were naturists—they liked to be naked. All the guests had to be naked too. They re-enacted the sort of thing found in the Roman Empire, where such baths were part of everyday life. In the building was a large pool for lounging about and swimming in, but there were other rooms with various purposes, hot rooms, cold rooms, you know the sort of thing.

Maggie hired young people to act as the slaves. They would rub scented oils into the guests' skin and scrape it off with special tools copied from roman originals. Of course, there was wine, not just Italian wines, thankfully and there was music and dancing and frolicking as you might expect, but, amazingly, no sex was allowed! No guests stayed overnight. It all finished at midnight."

"What? No SEX—you must be kidding me again, Len!"

'No, Rudi, the chief constable who used to go to these affairs, with his wife in tow, said it was an absolute rule. NO sex! Actually, we were told that the romans separated the sexes in the baths, too. No mixing. They had different time slots, apparently."

"Wow!"

"But, you see, that was how the Romans used the baths back in history. There was no coupling then, either, apparently. It was just a way of life back then."

"Well, would you believe it?"

"As a psychiatrist, you would be interested in the fact that neither Maggie nor Simon had ever, as far as could be gathered, bothered with dating the opposite or even the same, sex. They both seemed to be totally asexual."

"Yes, that is indeed very interesting, Len. Can we have a look inside of those buildings?"

"Afraid not, my friend, all boarded up and secure. We were allowed to search for bodies and forensic evidence but that was strictly controlled and revealed nothing of value. No sign of recent occupation or imprisonment. A security firm has been hired by the lawyers and nothing must be touched until the estate's future has been sorted out.

The lawyers think and I agree, that what will probably happen eventually is that the whole thing will be sold off, lock, stock and barrel. The family fortune is proving to be another great mystery, but that is not our province. It will take many years to sort. No, this is where our tour ends. We must go back to the station."

"What if Natalie is incarcerated in the cellars under the main house, Len, have you thought of that."

"Don't go there, Rudi. It is too ghastly to contemplate. Come, let's go."

Chapter Nine

Three Weeks Previously

Simon waited, nervously, for his invited guest to arrive. The woman who looked just like his mother. She WAS his mother! Alive again! The woman in the gold dress, who said her name was 'Maggie'. He had thought of nothing else ever since the Ball, last Saturday night. A night that must have changed everything. What had Fate got in store for him? What magic had transformed his life forever? However he tried, he could not work out what had happened. Did it really happen? Will Maggie come?

His whole body was trembling with excitement. He said to himself, "Yes, I deserve this! Something or someone has planned this to happen. I am destined to be reunited with my mother. It is happening as it was written in the stars. It is my Destiny!"

He thought, "That's why the other two girls died. Of course! It wasn't my fault! Not my fault! It was just not in my destiny. That was it!"

The buzzer at the gates sounded loudly. Simon rushed to the control panel on the wall and pressed the appropriate button to open the gates. The CCTV showed two ladies rather than the one he was expecting, but he recognised the taller of the two as the woman in the gold dress. He was really upset that she had brought a companion with her, but it was better than nothing. He would think of a way to get Maggie alone with him.

Very soon the car pulled up outside, where Simon was waiting at the entrance to his home. He lost no time ushering the two women inside, taking them to the grandest of the several reception rooms, the one at the rear of the house, which led out into the Victorian Orangery/Conservatory. A beautiful room, with contemporary Arts and Crafts influences. Sumptuous in the extreme.

Simon, dressed to kill in a tweed suit, motioned for the two ladies to sit down, where they pleased.

Maggie said, "Lovely to see you again, Simon. I hope you don't mind, I've brought my younger sister Dawn with me, she insisted on coming with me and when she insists on something she generally gets what she wants!"

"That's fine. Welcome to you both. Now, what would you both like to drink?"

Simon looked uncomfortable acting as the host. He turned to Maggie first and said, "Maggie?" who replied "Scotch would be nice. A large one, please."

Simon turned to Dawn, "And for you—?" The girl looked and sounded very wound-up and tense.

'Dawn' spoke, through gritted teeth. "Tell me, Simon, where is Natalie?"

'Maggie' (Pat) looked at her with alarm. She said, "What are you doing?"

Simon went white. He looked unable to speak. This reaction, to Melissa's mind (for that, of course, was who

'Dawn' really was) proved conclusively that the man was guilty.

"WHERE IS SHE? WHERE IS MY SISTER, YOU FUCKING BASTARD!"

Simon fell to his knees, sobbing hysterically.

Melissa went over to him and kicked him, hard.

"WHERE IS NATALIE? TELL ME! YOU SWINE!"

Simon wailed. "She is dead. I told you. It was an accident. I didn't mean to kill her. It just happened."

"WHERE IS HER BODY?" Melissa screamed.

Simon's face suddenly changed. He looked like a demon. He laughed hysterically. He yelled, "I CUT HER UP! SHE IS IN THE SEPTIC TANK. YOU WILL NEVER LEAVE MY HOUSE ALIVE. I WILL KILL YOU BOTH." He pushed at Melissa and started to rise to his feet, menacingly.

There was a crash as two masked men burst into the room from the Conservatory. But they were too late to stop Melissa. She pulled a pistol out of her bag and shot Simon in the middle of his forehead. The young girl then fainted and collapsed on top of Simon's body.

Pat rushed over to Melissa and moved her away from the body of Simon. She turned to her husband, Ian and Ben her boss. "I had no idea Melissa was thinking of doing this, I did not know she had a gun. She never told me. I should have stopped her—"

Ian had checked out Simon's condition. He shook his head. "This man is dead. The bullet was fired point blank into his brain."

Ben said, calmly, "Let's all take a spell to sort this mess out. We are where we are. A murder has been committed here and we are all involved. So we need to clear up this mess and clear out PDQ. Suggestions?"

"Should we call the police?" asked Pat.

Both men shook their heads. As ex-members of the Royal Navy's Special Boat Squad, the equivalent of the Army's SAS, they had been in many tight, dangerous situations in the past, serving their Queen and Country. Like all SBS men and women, they were quiet, efficient and above all, **ruthless**. They were very used to dealing with dead bodies, as servicemen and in a civilian context, as private detectives.

Ben, as a RN Commander had outranked Ian, who had been more a technician and intelligence officer with the nominal rank of a Lieutenant. Ben was a natural born leader of men, fearless and bold in combat and he knew he was expected to take a lead now.

Ian said, "We need to clear up and get the hell out of here, mate! We can worry about the rights and wrongs at a later date."

Ben said, "Exactly! I know what to do. But we must, as a first step, check the house from top to bottom to make sure no one else is here. You and me, Ian, at the double. Pat needs to stay with Mel. Come on!"

The two men raced around the house, checking every room for signs of life. They found nothing. As they had initially judged, there was only Simon in the house when they arrived.

Slightly breathless, not as fit as they were, they returned to find Pat. Melissa had not regained consciousness.

Pat said, "I think she is alright. She's breathing OK and her pulse is strong. She was just overcome by emotion and stress, but we need to get her home soon."

"Yes, well, Pat you take Mel back to your home with you in your car—now! Call an ambulance when you get there. Just in case."

Ben lifted Mel as easily as if she weighed nothing and carried her out to Pat's car. Ian had no trouble in operating the electronics to open the gates as the car swept smoothly away down the long driveway.

Ben said, "Ian—there's only one way of making sure there is no forensic evidence for the police to find and I'm sure you know what that is?"

"Fire."

"Of course. See if you can find some matches, Ian, I'll pile up some wooden and fabric bits and pieces in the middle of the floor. I've got the gun."

In a few minutes, Ian returned bearing a gas barbecue lighter. Ben, who had smashed up some of the beautiful furniture meanwhile, lit the bonfire. The two men watched the blaze take hold. Satisfied, they quickly left the building. As said, "quiet, efficient, Ruthless!"

Chapter Ten

Later that evening Ben and Ian arrived back at Ian and Pat's house. They had left their car in a country lane at the rear of Simon's property, on a grass verge. They had followed Pat and Melissa's car part of the way and then left them and found the parking place they required.

From their clandestine forays into enemy territory in their service for their Queen and Country, they were trained and ready to gain access to Simon's estate. Ian easily disabled the electronic intruder net protecting the estate, it had been his speciality, so alarms were not a problem.

They had entered the conservatory at the back of the house just about the same time as Simon had led the two ladies into his main reception room. They had been listening intently to the conversations taking place, so when they heard Simon yelling that he was going to kill the two visitors, they had no choice but to burst into the room, too late, however, to stop Mel killing Simon.

The two men found there was an ambulance outside the house, so they quietly entered, Ian calling his wife's name. Pat replied, "In here, Ian!" so they joined the paramedics and Pat in the front lounge. One of the paramedics, a middle-aged man, seemed to be in charge. He said to Ian, "Are you a relative of the patient, sir?"

Ian replied, "No, she is just a friend. We have been helping her with a problem she had. How is she? She suddenly collapsed."

"Well, she's not in any danger, sir, but we have been unable to bring her round, so we are just in the process of taking her with us to the A&E. I don't think it's so much physical as mental, sir. They'll need to do a few tests."

"Oh, dear! Right, Well, I'll go with her, then."

Both Ian and Ben were just wearing jeans and black tee-shirts. The paramedics looked at the two of them rather oddly but asked no questions. It wasn't their job.

Pat said, "No, you two men stay here. I'll go with Mel."

The ambulance men loaded Melissa onto a stretcher and carried her outside. Pat whispered, "I had no idea about the gun, you know—Mel told me she was going to confront Simon and try to get him to confess to abducting her sister with me as a witness. That was the plan I thought."

She pulled a face, then added, "I'll get my coat. God knows when I'll be back. You two have got a lot to talk about! I'll ring when there's any news."

She hugged and kissed Ian, then rushed away.

Ian grabbed a whisky bottle and glasses and the two men sat down and each drank a long pull, saying nothing.

After a few minutes, Ian broke the silence.

He said, "You know, Ben, I think Mel is in trouble, she's blown a fuse, to put it crudely. I've seen a similar thing when we were fighting terrorists in Iraq. I've known men to suddenly just keel over like Mel did and it was months before they even started to speak again. A complete mental breakdown. I'm really worried about that girl, she is so young and to kill somebody like that—really traumatic for her."

"Not so much fun for Simon, either—" said Ben, sardonically.

"Will the body be found, then"

"I rather doubt it, not for ages, with all that house rubble piled on top of it."

They both took another long draught of the golden liquid.

"If so, I imagine the police will be coming to interview her. She and her mum and dad must be suspects," said Ian.

"And if they do, they may find out she was a client of ours and will come knocking on our door, too."

"Correct. Such larks, Pip!"

"We better fix on our story, then, mate!"

"Not tonight. Anything on the telly?"

"Let's see. Any good murder stories, I wonder?"

At midnight, Pat returned. She had been told by the doctors that there was no point in her staying any longer. Melissa showed no signs of waking. She was in a deep coma. The doctors had said that she might wake up tonight or next week or—who knows? It was 'in the lap of the gods'.

Chapter Eleven

Present Day

Detective Inspector Michael Carter and newly-promoted Detective *Sergeant* Penelope Summers arrived, per appointment, at the Ellis's house.

Mike said, as the door was opened by Jessica Ellis, "So sorry to hear about your daughter, Melissa. How is she doing, any sign of her waking up yet?"

"No, nothing. It's dreadful. Both our daughters—but do come in, I'll make some coffee. David, my husband, is here, too, as requested."

"Great! Thanks a lot," said Penny. She had lost a lot of weight and looked fabulous.

The two coppers followed Jessica into the front lounge. David rose from his chair to greet them. He said, "Ah, right, you're here. Come and sit down where you like."

The four settled down opposite one another in the pleasant room, filled with sunshine, as though for a cosy chat between four friends.

Jessica went off to fetch coffee and while she was gone the conversation was just general, the weather, the recent weather, always a topic of interest in England, helpfully.

The coffee arrived, together with a large plate of tempting-looking biscuits and Jessica did the honours. Only both ladies abstained from the biscuits. Both David and Mike tucked in with two each on their plates. The atmosphere was relaxed.

Mike got down to business. He said, "I presume you have heard nothing more from the person who abducted your younger daughter, Natalie?"

David said, emphatically, "Not a word! We really have no idea what has happened to Natalie. It is quite devastating. No news certainly isn't good news, really. Have the police made any progress, yet?"

Mike noticed that Jessica had blushed furiously and this puzzled him. Was David lying? Was he hiding something?

He said, "I wish I could tell you that we had made progress, but that would be a lie. The short answer is that we haven't any more idea now than on day one of the investigation. We have really tried hard and explored several avenues of investigation but all without any success at all. I am so sorry, Mr and Mrs Ellis, I really am."

Mike's handsome, boyish features looked so doleful that Jessica felt sorry for the man. Her colour had still not returned to normal. Mike felt he had to ask, "Are you all right, Mrs Ellis? Is there something you would like to tell us?"

Jessica gulped and looked desperately at her husband. He got up and patted her hand. "She's very upset about the whole thing, of course, that's all it is. Don't worry inspector, we have no news to tell you. Well—actually there is *something*—we have decided to sell this house, too many memories, you know, we are moving far away from here so that there will be nothing to see to remind us of our dreadful losses.

Of course, we will move Melissa too, to a care home close to where we are going, in Spain, actually. So my poor wife has that to cope with too, you see. She will have to sell off her business, the stables, the horses. It's a huge move, but it's better than sitting here in this empty house staring at the walls. Once we are settled everything will be much better, I'm sure."

Penny said, "Gosh! That is unexpected news. But what about if Natalie is found safe and well or if she just turns up out of the blue, what then?"

"I am convinced that won't happen. My wife and I have given up all hope that Natalie is alive. Parents *know*, you know. It is strange but true. No, officers, that isn't a worry."

Jessica got up and rushed out of the room. Penny made as if to follow her, but David stopped her, he said, "No, leave her be. She's fine, don't worry. Just upset." Penny reluctantly sat down again.

"More coffee?" asked David, brightly.

Mike said, "I don't think there's any point in continuing this any further, Mr Ellis. We'll leave you in peace and let you know just as soon as we have any further news, should there be any."

The two coppers got up and rather abruptly left, but in the car on the way back to the station they were both very quiet and thoughtful. Penny broke the silence, she said, "What do you think of all that, sir?"

Mike cleared his throat, "I'm bloody worried, Pen. They are lying and hiding something. I am sure of it. I can only guess at what it might be. What do you think, Pen, you're good at this kind of thing?"

"It's David. He's dominating his wife. He really tried to hush her up there and that was obvious. She does not agree with what is happening at all that much is plain."

"What if Simon paid up that million pounds compensation, Pen and David does not want the police to know about it?"

"That's exactly what I'm thinking too! It would explain everything, wouldn't it—the move to Spain, for example, I mean, where would they get the money to do that?"

"Taking Melissa over there, the cost of care over there, hellish expensive, surely. They must know Natalie is dead, surely they would not leave that house if they thought she was still alive. It does not make sense."

Mike steered the car back into the station parking area. They sat there for a short while, staring into space.

Mike said, "Well, God knows what we can do about it. It beats me. Now that Rudi has returned to the States, we can't run it past him. I'll have a word with the boss. Come on Pen. On with the Motley!"

Mike gave his report to the Superintendent without delay. Len listened without comment until Mike had finished.

Len said, "What about Melissa, Mike? How is she progressing, have you contacted the hospital for an update?"

"Not for a while. The last time I enquired they gave me the same answer they always give—she is physically perfect, not in any danger, but deeply comatose with no sign of ever recovering. She is not brain dead as such and there is nothing about switching off life support as she is not in need of life support. She needs a lot of looking after of course. It's really difficult, feeding, cleaning her up, treating for bed sores, almost a full-time job looking after her."

195

"Melissa came to see you some weeks ago. Tell me again what that was all about, Mike?"

Mike coloured up slightly. He felt so guilty about lying to his boss. He saw the superintendent's eyes boring into his soul.

"Er, she just wanted to know what we were doing. Er, you know, what progress we had made, that sort of thing. Nothing really."

Len continued staring at him.

"You're not telling me the whole truth, are you, Mike." He said, softly.

"Christ!"

"Come on, out with it."

Mike burst into tears.

Len got up and gently placed his hand on the young man's shoulder.

"Don't be upset. Tell me what is worrying you. I won't bite, you know. I have every confidence in you, Inspector, whatever it is, I'll understand that you acted as you thought best at the time."

"Mike gulped and got out his handkerchief and blew his nose."

"I'll be glad to get it off my chest, sir."

"Go on, lad," Len whispered, gently.

"She wanted to know who was our prime suspect and I told her it was Simon Shaw. She told me she was hiring a private detective who could investigate in ways not open to the police. I was sure it was Simon who abducted her sister and I hated been warned off about investigating that guy, by those on high. So I told her. You will have my letter of resignation on your desk first thing in the morning sir."

"Ah. I rather thought it was something like that. Thank you, Mike. I won't hear of you resigning. You are a good man doing his best. What more can I ask of anyone. I will take no action about this, Mike. But we must consider again who murdered Simon in the light of this.

That interview with Melissa need not come out. It will be just you and I. Take some time off, Mike. Go home. It's no problem. You broke a lot of rules, but for the best of reasons. I salute your courage and your motives. Tomorrow morning we will start work. Bright and Early, My Office!"

Mike wished he could hug his boss, but he knew better. He got up, nodded his head in gratitude and walked quickly out of the office. He felt two stones lighter. On his way home he broke into tears again and had to stop the car for a while, but by the time he was home, he was fine.

His wife greeted him in surprise, "You're early. Had a good day, dear?"

"Fantastic!"

Chapter Twelve

The next morning, bright and early, Len and Mike were together in Len's office. Rudi's desk was sadly empty. Everyone missed the guy. He really did light up a room.

Len noticed Mike looking at the desk. He said, "I rang him last night, well it was morning for him. He's on his way back. He doesn't want to miss this. He will be back here tomorrow."

"Crikey Moses! That's good news!"

Len grinned. "It certainly is!"

He poured a cup of coffee for each of them, from his private coffee-making machine, which used little bought plastic pots of coffee and was delicious.

When they were settled, Len said, "Now, you said Melissa told you she was hiring a private detective to help solve the case of her missing sister, Natalie. We really need to know who this was. Do you know?"

"Oh yes, I insisted on knowing this. It is a firm called B&I Private Investigators. I did make some enquiries about the firm. It is based in Wolverhampton and Manchester, so is quite a big firm, but it only really has three detectives on the staff who move from one branch to another as needed, sir."

"Names?" Len was writing in longhand with a fountain pen on lined paper. An old-fashioned detective, but one of the best. No tablets for him!

"Boss is Benjamin McGuire, partner is Ian Jones and the third partner is Ian Jones's wife, Patricia Jones."

"Go on. What else do have you found out about this firm?"

"Well, apparently the boss, Ben McGuire is using his wife's maiden name because he is actually Lord Ben Hawke, Earl of Somerton, retired from the Royal Navy, well, invalided out, who decided he fancied being a P.I! His partner in crime Ian Jones was a colleague of his in Her Majesty's service and ex-Lieutenant. His wife, Patricia was hired as a receptionist but she now is also a partner and an active detective, to boot. They have a good reputation in the field. That's about all I know, sir."

"Sounds good. Make an appointment and you and I will go and have a word with these characters, Mike. Should be interesting. Perhaps we'll invite Rudi along, too. Then it will be three on three."

Chapter Thirteen

The private nursing home where Melissa Ellis was being cared-for was quiet and peaceful one night shortly afterwards. The girl was in a small room, on a special waterbed. The light was dim. She was hooked up to several tubes serving her bodily needs. She was breathing normally, her chest rising and falling as it had now for many months.

She looked rather pretty, as the nurses always made sure her hair was washed and combed neatly and did up her face with a little rouge and foundation 'serum'. Sometimes her mum, Jessica, spent a whole day sitting by her side, reading aloud a novel and talking to her comatose daughter as if she was fully conscious.

Her dad, David, had seldom visited. It upset him too much, he said, truthfully, but he was rather glad he was not having to explain to his daughter how he was investing the 'blood money', as she described it, viciously. The money was now safely in a bank in Jersey, in the Channel Islands, where tax was really low for millionaires. He had invested really well and was making a fortune. He was, of course, a financial expert.

That evening, suddenly, Melissa's eyes first flickered, then opened wide. She tried to scream, unsuccessfully. The machine she was connected to started to sound an alarm and a night nurse rushed in to see what was happening. She immediately realised that Melissa was awake and beginning to thrash around on the bed, with her mouth opened in a silent scream.

The nurse, a middle-aged and experienced practitioner took control at once. She pressed down on the patient's shoulders and talked to her soothingly.

"You're alright, darling, don't struggle, you'll hurt yourself. You are quite safe in hospital, my dear, you have been asleep for a long time, but you are now conscious and that is wonderful news. Your parents will be over the moon…"

The nurse, name of Mason, continued talking to the girl as she held a glass of water to her lips. She had pressed a button on entering to summon a doctor, of course and one now appeared, a tall young man, rather dishevelled, who had obviously been having a nap.

"Goodness!" he said. "I'm amazed! I can't say I have much experience of this, but, you know, there's nothing physically wrong with you. Now you are awake I'll make some arrangements to get you back on your feet. We'll have to get rid of all your intubations of course, plus you'll probably need some physio and a few tests, but really this is great. Welcome back to the land of the living young lady!"

He turned to the nurse. "See if you can get some more water down her, Nurse Mason, please."

The nurse continued holding the girl's shoulders and she gradually settled down and became quiet. Her eyes started to focus and she gulped another drink. "My throat's sore!" she croaked.

"Well, of course, it is. You haven't had a drink for many months. Keep sipping the water and try and collect your thoughts. Can you tell me your name?"

"Melissa Ellis."

"That's fine. Now, what do you remember about what happened to you, my lovely?"

"I remember. I killed a man. I shot him in his head with a gun. He killed my sister." She said this quite calmly, her voice growing stronger. She smiled proudly.

"You've been dreaming, sweetheart! I'm sure you haven't done any such thing. Look, try to get some sleep, even though you've been unconscious for such a long time, waking up can be very stressful. Just rest for a while quietly. We'll sort you out properly in the morning."

"I need to speak to Detective Inspector Carter. Where's my phone?"

Chapter Fourteen

Chief Superintendent Len Rowles, together with his good friend Dr Rudi Valentine and Detective Sergeant Penelope Summers arrived promptly at the offices of the B&J Detective Agency, having made a telephoned appointment. Rudi had offered to take notes at the meeting, for his own use, as he was writing a book about the case, as well as for the police.

The three investigators entered the agency offices in Wolverhampton, dressed formally in business suits, including Penny who looked rather gorgeous. She was in the lead and she approached Pat Jones, who was acting as receptionist. Pat looked smart but severe in appearance. Hardly any make-up, hair scraped back, black suit and cream shirt buttoned up to the neck.

She had done this to make sure the visitors would not consider her being the mysterious and glamorous 'Maggie' who was such a sensation in her gold dress, at the ball. The three PIs had discussed how to tackle a police interview at some length and had carefully prepared their response.

Pat asked Penny how she could help.

Penny said, "This is Chief Superintendent Rowles, Dr Valentine who is helping us from the FBI and I am Detective Sergeant Summers. I believe we are expected."

Penny and the two men all held up their IDs.

Pat pretended to look at a register on her desk.

"Oh yes. Very well. Please take a seat and I will contact Mr McGuire and Mr Jones and tell them you are here. Help yourself to coffee if you wish." She indicated where they were with a delicate hand.

Pat then picked up the phone on her desk and said the necessary information, then replaced it and turned back to her laptop computer screen, ignoring the visitors.

Several minutes passed. Len was not amused. He stood up and approached the receptionists' desk menacingly, but just then the equally huge figure of Ben McGuire opened the door of his office and advanced, a smile on his steely, black-bearded face.

"Do come in gentlemen and er, lady, sorry to keep you waiting."

The office was simple. Modern office fittings of a conventional type. Ben went and sat at his desk and indicated that the three visitors should sit, facing him. He continued to smile.

He said, "My word! Quite a high-powered group. What on earth can you be wanting from us?"

Len said he would take the lead. He said. "We are conducting a murder investigation, Mr McGuire and the murdered person was a rich and powerful man with friends in high places, as they say. That is the reason why such high-ranking officers are involved in this case."

"And who would this murdered person be and what connection has he got with our little agency, may I ask?"

"Does the name Simon Shaw mean anything to you?"

"Rings a bell. Wait a minute, I'll bring my partner, Ian Jones in. He may be able to jog my memory. Simon Shaw, you say?"

He got up and left the room, coming back instantly with a tall and handsome colleague, who entered and shook hands with the visitors. A charming man, thought Penny. Ben introduced his partner, saying, "Ian is the brains of our agency, you know. I am more physical."

Ben addressed Ian. "The Chief Superintendent would like to know if we have any connection with a murdered man they are investigating, name of Simon Shaw. It rings a bell with me but I can't quite place the guy."

"Simon Shaw," Ian pretended to search his memory. "Ah, yes—he's the guy who was on the news a while ago. Body found in his burnt-out mansion in Shropshire. Is that the guy? I didn't realise he had been murdered though. The media did not report that as far as I remember."

Len said, "Yes. That's the guy. We understand that your firm was involved in trying to bring this man, who was a person of interest to the police, to what the sister of a girl, allegedly abducted by Dr Shaw, to justice. I am pretty sure that the sister of the abducted girl hired your agency for this purpose."

"Really! And what is the name of this girl you say hired our agency?"

"Her name, as I think you know, is Melissa Ellis, sister of Natalie Ellis who was abducted and probably killed some months ago."

Ben said, "Hang on," he looked amazed and puzzled. He rang through to reception. "Pat, love, did we act for a Miss Melissa Ellis at all?" He listened for a while and then his face pretended to clear. "Oh, that girl. Yes, I remember now. Well, I'll be damned!"

"Sorry about that. Yes, we were approached by that girl, some weeks back with some weird and wonderful plan to unmask Simon Shaw. Of course. You remember, Ian, I told you about it at the time."

Ian nodded his head, vigorously.

"That's right, Ben. But I don't think we took that case on, did we. It's not the sort of thing we do at all. Sorry, Chief Superintendent, that's all there was to it."

"Mm. Look, as I say, this is a murder inquiry. We could insist on seeing all your records." Len was growing angry.

"Insist away, old chap. We have nothing to hide. You are welcome."

Len thundered, "We will get to the bottom of this, one way or another."

"So, this Melissa, what does she say, Superintendent?"

"Unfortunately, she is unable to speak. She is in a coma, as I think you probably know."

"What a shame. Poor girl, mind you, she seemed a bit unbalanced by her desire for revenge. Fantasising. I felt sorry for her at the time, now I think back."

Rudi took over. He said, "Look, guys, there's something else. There was a ball, given by a local aristocrat and you, Ben, we know attended this ball. I suppose you remember that occasion?"

"Yes, I do—but what that has got to do with anything I can't imagine."

"You were seen with a remarkably beautiful and glamorous woman on your arm and she could be the key to this investigation."

"Nonsense. She was just an old friend of my wife, who was staying with us for a few days. She was bored out of her mind and insisted I took her to that damned ball. That's all it was."

"We were told by witnesses who were present that Simon Shaw was at the ball and was completely knocked out by that lady. We were told she resembled his mother, another gorgeous female who died in an accident and that Simon invited her to his house, possibly on the night of the fire and the murder. That is why you are connected to this case, sir."

"Ridiculous! Maggie LeBon was just an old friend from Dublin University. My wife is Irish and she lives there all week, joining me here on weekends. My wife owns a large company in Dublin and is generally busy over there—it was difficult for her having Maggie as a guest.

She had not seen her for years and now she is touring Africa—she is an inveterate traveller, so she told us. I am sure she did not visit this Simon Shaw chap. She left us the next day after the ball and we have not heard from her since. Nor have we any particular desire to contact her. She is an exhausting person to be with."

Len growled under his breath. Penny kept quiet.

Rudi, however, was not finished. He looked relaxed and gave Len and Ian the benefit of one of his 1000-watt smiles.

He said, "I'll tell you what happened. You, Mr McGuire and your partner, Mr Jones, ex-Navy commandoes, went along with an actress you hired to play the part of Simon Shaw's mother. A mother he idolised and was obsessed about. You used this actress to gain access to Simon's mansion. I think she took along Melissa, posing as a friend along for company.

I've been to the Shaw's mansion and I know how difficult it is to gain entry, but he willingly opened his gates for Maggie and Melissa and you two guys snuck in behind her. When the two women were shown into the house, I believe Melissa confronted Simon accusing him of murdering Natalie, her sister. I think Simon attacked the two women, but Melissa had taken a gun which she produced and shot Simon dead.

I think, hearing the shot, you two guys rushed in but too late. I don't think you knew Melissa had a gun and was going to kill Simon. You thought she might wring a confession from him and you would be witnesses. But the murder happened. You would all be accessories to murder. Equally guilty and sent down for Life.

So you then set fire to the house to destroy any evidence and cooked up the story you have just told me. I know you will deny this, of course you will, but I reckon that is more or less what happened."

"Really? You should write fairy stories for a living, sir, that's all I can say!" said Ian, calmly.

Len got up. "You've not heard the last of this!" he thundered.

He stormed out, followed by the grinning Rudi and the rather dumbfounded sergeant who had said nothing at all.

Ben looked at Ian. Ian looked at Ben. Pat, who had been listening to it all, came in looking concerned.

She said, "My God, that Dr Valentine fellow was good, wasn't he? But he has no evidence, has he?"

Ben said, "Don't worry, Pat. They know when they are beaten. But, as you say, that guy was good."

"What if Melissa comes round and confesses though?"

"I've thought of that. They won't believe her for one minute, despite what that yank said. It's just too fanciful for words, it would be laughed out of court and they know it."

Chapter Fifteen

Melissa's father and mother rushed around to the hospital, overwhelmed with joy at the news. Within a few days, Melissa was at home, but she was not the same girl she used to be. She was pale and drawn and spoke very little. She kept saying she wanted to call the police but did not make much effort to insist on it. Her phone had gone missing. She seemed almost zombie-like, unresponsive, not eating much at all, not doing anything but just lying on her bed, staring into space.

David, in an effort to liven the girl, told her of his plans for them all to go and live in Spain. At first, she seemed unable to comprehend. Then, something inside her clicked.

"What's happened with all that gold? All that blood money!" she yelled at her dad.

"You know what we agreed. It was to find out what happened to Natalie and to bring her abductor to justice. You hired a private detective and went off all over the place for weeks. You didn't tell us anything about what you were doing. But that is why I invested all that money so that we could afford to hire the detectives, you remember, love, you must do."

"So you invested the gold, Daddy, that's what you did?" There was a look of horror on the daughter's face.

"Yes, darling, that's right. Surely we should see this as something positive to come out of the horror of Natalie's abduction. We deserve this money and we will use it to make ours and many other people's lives better for it. Can't you see that? We can do so much good to counter all the evil."

"I see." Melissa's face was pale and set. "I'm going out for a while," she said. "Breath of fresh air."

"That's fine, darling," said a relieved father.

Melissa took her father's car keys and left the house. She got into the car and went straight round to the police station, where she asked to see DI Carter.

"There's a girl to see you, sir," said the receptionist. "Just says her name is Melissa."

"Ouch!" said Mike. "Gosh, better send her into my office, Mavis, please."

When the girl appeared, Mike was standing waiting for her.

He said, "Wow! I've heard you have recovered from your coma, but I didn't expect to see you this soon, Miss Ellis. Please come and sit down and tell me what's bothering you."

"Thank you, Inspector. Remember the last time I came to see you, you told me, privately, about Dr Shaw being your prime suspect in your investigation into what happened to my sister?"

"Well, of course, yes, I do remember. I hope you haven't told anybody about that, apart from the private detectives you hired to help you. I know you went to see them, but my boss tells me they did not take your case on?"

"Oh, I see." Melissa thought for a moment, then continued. "That is what B&I told you, then. Right. Well that's absolutely right, Inspector, absolutely right."

"Plus you must have heard that Dr Shaw is dead?"

"Well, that is what I have come about. It was me that killed him. I shot him in the head. It was after that that I must have blown a fuse or something and went into a coma for five months or so."

"You killed him, you say?" Mike said calmly.

"Yes, I killed him and I'm glad I did, but now I must face the consequences of what I did. I cannot live with this on my mind. I will make a full confession and do whatever you want. I will plead guilty and will serve my time. I am quite determined about this. So arrest me, Inspector and lock me up. I have no desire to go back home."

"I'm afraid I can't do that, Miss Ellis. Frankly, I don't believe you. You are ill and you are fantasising. Go home to your family and get yourself better."

Melissa looked angrily at the young inspector. "I can prove I did it! I'll tell you exactly how I did it."

"Well, for a start, how did you gain access to Dr Shaw's residence? It is like Fort Knox there, I know. So tell me, how did you get in to see him?"

"Er, I just rang the bell outside the gates and he let me in."

"That's rubbish. I know for a fact he would not even have answered you if you just arrived at his house and pressed the bell. Sorry, but that's nonsense. Look, do you know how many other people have confessed to killing the doctor? I'll tell you—seventeen. Whenever there's a crime such as this, with media coverage, a lot of people come here to confess. All of them fantasising, like yourself."

"I'm not fantasising. I am determined to do this. I will stay here until you arrest me for murder. I'll go above your head if I must."

Mike looked serious. He said, "Listen—if I were to arrest you and charge you and if you, as you say, can prove you did it, do you realise what that will mean, not just to you and your family, but to me, my wife and two little children, for giving you that information, also to the private detectives, for I know they are lying and you are lying about their involvement."

"You could not have gained access without their help and I know about the ball and the mythical Maggie you used as a decoy. They will all be charged as accessories to murder. Two or maybe three more families, lives ruined, and why? To make you feel better? You have saved the lives of several other young girls from the clutches of a psychological monster preying on young girls for some crazy quest to replace the mother he idolised."

"You have had your revenge. Be satisfied. Go on home and live your life as a nurse, helping hundreds or thousands of patients recover from illness. Devote your life to that if you want to feel better, rather than spending many years in a prison cell. At least go and think about the consequences for a day or two, before pushing this confession again. Please. For my two little girls, for a start. You will, by your confession, ruin their lives, for I will probably go to prison and they will lose their daddy. Just for helping you."

Melissa said nothing. She got up swiftly and left the room. She got into her father's car and did not fasten her seatbelt. She drove at top speed down the main road and then deliberately crashed into a solid brick wall. She died instantly, thrown through the windscreen headfirst into the wall.

Some days later, when all had settled, Len and Rudi sat in his lounge, finishing off the last whisky of the night. Rudi was going home the next day. The murder of Simon Shaw had been shelved indefinitely for lack of evidence.

Len said, "I'll really miss these chats we've had, Rudi, old friend. Thank you for the offer of me visiting you in the summer and I really look forward to that. I reckon you'll have finished that book you are writing about the mad doctor and the shocking Kylie and Natalie cases?"

"Sure will, Len. Though it takes an age to get a book published y'know. Even for an established author such as me. Actually, I've decided to turn that case into a fictional psychological crime thriller, rather than my usual students' texts."

"Oh, right. Good idea. So what will you call your novel, then, Rudi?" He swallowed the last of his whisky. The cat on his lap turned on his back and purred loudly, hoping for a tummy tickle.

Rudi thought for a while. He lifted the cat on his lap into the air, where it looked sleepily at him, wondering what was happening.

He smiled, lighting up the room. "I think I'll call it '**The Girl on the Bike**'."

THE END

Len, Mike, Penny and Rudi will return!